Emily Harvale lives in East Sussex, in the UK – although she would prefer to live in the French Alps ... or Canada ... or anywhere that has several months of snow. Emily loves snow almost as much as she loves Christmas.

Having worked in the City (London) for several years, Emily returned to her home town of Hastings where she spends her days writing ... and wondering if it will ever snow.

You can contact her via her website, Facebook or Instagram.

There is also a Facebook group where fans can chat with Emily about her books, her writing day and life in general. Details can be found on Emily's website.

Author contacts:
www.emilyharvale.com
www.twitter.com/emilyharvale
www.facebook.com/emilyharvalewriter
www.instagram.com/emilyharvale

GW00771815

Scan the code above to see all Emily's books on Amazon

Also by this author

The Golf Widows' Club
Sailing Solo
Carole Singer's Christmas
Christmas Wishes
A Slippery Slope
The Perfect Christmas Plan
Be Mine
It Takes Two
Bells and Bows on Mistletoe Row

Lizzie Marshall series:
Highland Fling – book 1
Lizzie Marshall's Wedding – book 2

Goldebury Bay series:
Ninety Days of Summer – book 1
Ninety Steps to Summerhill – book 2
Ninety Days to Christmas – book 3

Hideaway Down series:
A Christmas Hideaway – book 1
Catch A Falling Star – book 2
Walking on Sunshine – book 3
Dancing in the Rain – book 4

Hall's Cross series
Deck the Halls – book 1
The Starlight Ball – book 2

Michaelmas Bay series
Christmas Secrets in Snowflake Cove – book 1
Blame it on the Moonlight – book 2

Lily Pond Lane series
The Cottage on Lily Pond Lane – four-part serial
Part One – New beginnings
Part Two – Summer secrets
Part Three – Autumn leaves

Part Four – Trick or treat
Christmas on Lily Pond Lane
Return to Lily Pond Lane
A Wedding on Lily Pond Lane
Secret Wishes and Summer Kisses on Lily Pond Lane

Wyntersleap series
Christmas at Wynter House – Book 1
New Beginnings at Wynter House – Book 2
A Wedding at Wynter House – Book 3
Love is in the Air – spin off

Merriment Bay series
Coming Home to Merriment Bay – Book 1
(four-part serial)
Part One – A Reunion
Part Two – Sparks Fly
Part Three – Christmas
Part Four – Starry Skies
Chasing Moonbeams in Merriment Bay – Book 2
Wedding Bells in Merriment Bay – Book 3

Seahorse Harbour series
Summer at my Sister's – book 1
Christmas at Aunt Elsie's – book 2
Just for Christmas – book 3
Tasty Treats at Seahorse Bites Café – book 4
Dreams and Schemes at The Seahorse Inn – book 5
Weddings and Reunions in Seahorse Harbour – book 6

Clementine Cove series
Christmas at Clementine Cove – book 1
Broken Hearts and Fresh Starts at Cove Café – book 2
Friendships Blossom in Clementine Cove – book 3

Norman Landing series
Saving Christmas – book 1
A not so secret Winter Wedding – book 2
Sunsets and surprises at Seascape Café-book 3
A Date at the end of The Pier – book 4

ISBN 978-1-917227-13-1

Published by Crescent Gate Publishing

Print edition published worldwide 2025
E-edition published worldwide 2025

Cover design by JR and Emily Harvale

Acknowledgements

My grateful thanks go to the following:

My webmaster, David Cleworth who does so much more than website stuff.
My cover design team, JR.
Luke Brabants. Luke is a talented artist and can be found at: www.lukebrabants.com
My wonderful friends for their friendship and love. You know I love you all.
All the fabulous members of my Readers' Club. You help and support me in so many ways and I am truly grateful for your ongoing friendship. I wouldn't be where I am today without you.
My Twitter and Facebook friends, and fans of my Facebook author page. It's great to chat with you. You help to keep me (relatively) sane!

For Bruno. RIP.

Emily Harvale

A Week in Midwinter

CRESCENT GATE PUBLISHING

One

'You've booked a last-minute romantic break for you and Ted?'

The look of incredulity on my best friend, Erin's, face didn't exactly fill me with confidence as I paid for our hot drinks and we headed towards the one vacant table in The Corner Café, our favourite meeting place to catch up with each other's news.

I should've waited until we sat down before I told her, but I was excited, and I'll admit, more than a little anxious about my spur-of-the-moment booking. I couldn't keep it to myself any longer and I blurted it out the moment she joined me in the queue.

Momentarily lost for words, I nodded and forced a smile

'Do you actually *know* your boyfriend?' A deep frown replaced Erin's previous expression and her perfectly shaped brows knit together as she pulled out a chair and draped her bright blue faux fur jacket over the back of it.

All my doubts came flooding back, and I tried to think of something brilliant to say in response as I removed my almost identical jacket – but in red – and hung mine on a hook on the wall beside our table.

We'd bought the jackets together in the January sales, laughing because so many people said we looked like twin sisters rather than best friends, and we'd agreed some years before that we should dress the same sometimes, just for fun.

It was true. We did look remarkably similar with our blonde hair and green eyes – an unusual combination as most blonde-haired people we knew had blue eyes. Erin said that was just one of the things that not only made us special, but meant we would always be best friends. My hair was a little shorter and more of a golden blonde than Erin's icy white, and my eyes had a hint of hazel whereas Erin's were emerald green. Plus, Erin was an inch or two taller, and one size larger than me, but from a distance, we looked virtually the same.

'I … I thought it would be … a lovely surprise.' I pulled out my chair and sat opposite her, brilliance having failed me, yet again.

Erin snorted derisively. 'It'll be a surprise all right, but as for lovely…' Her words trailed off as she shook her head and leant towards me, her long blonde ponytail swishing back and forth like a wagging finger. 'Have you gone completely mad, Lucy?' She stared at me as though she expected a serious answer to that question.

I managed a laugh, but even that sounded slightly maniacal, and when the small, wafer thin, chocolate heart sitting on top of my hot chocolate, sank beneath the mountain of whipped cream and disappeared, it was as if it had taken my own heart with it, along with all the remnants of my joy and excitement about my up-coming week away.

'You think I've made a mistake?' I mumbled, plunging my spoon into my drink to retrieve the chocolate heart, but it was only half its original size by the time I managed to scoop it out and it was more of a gooey blob than anything resembling a heart.

I usually removed the little chocolate token before it sank, The Corner Café having added wafer thin chocolate shapes to all its cream-topped beverages for as long as I could remember. Throughout the year, each one symbolised something related to the month, or a special occasion. The first two weeks in February had always been a chocolate heart. From the fifteenth onwards, it was usually a snowflake, or a cloud, or a raindrop, dependent upon the weather.

'A mistake?' Erin bit her chocolate heart in half, having removed hers from her own hot chocolate the moment she sat down, and she shook her head again. 'A mistake is an understatement. Unless you plan to go on this romantic break alone. You've been dating Ted for over a year. How many days has the man taken off work in that time?'

I glanced across the table and met her piercing green eyes. 'None.'

'And how many weekends has he worked even though his job only requires him to be in his office from Monday to Friday?'

'Erm. I'm not sure, exactly.'

That was a lie, and we both knew it. One of the things I sometimes moaned about to Erin was the number of hours my boyfriend spent working.

Ted was an accountant, and he was always in great demand. I had no idea accountants were so popular, until I started dating Ted. He checked his phone every few minutes, night, and day, and he received and sent more texts in one evening than I did in one week. It was the only thing we argued about. Well. Not exactly argued. Ted didn't argue. Politely disagreed about, would be more accurate.

'Ball park figure,' Erin demanded.

I shrugged pathetically. 'About half.'

Erin raised her brows and fixed me with

a hard stare.

'Okay,' I admitted grudgingly. 'Almost every weekend. But sometimes it's only one of the days. And sometimes only mornings. And, because he worked for most of Christmas and I only saw him briefly on Christmas Day, he promised me on New Year's Eve that he'd spend more time with me once the January deadline was over. That he'd make more time for our relationship. He even said we should try to find the time to go away together for a few days in February. So this week away will be perfect.'

Erin didn't seem convinced. 'Are you sure about that? The evidence so far is not looking good.'

Erin was a Detective Constable in one of the MITs (Major Investigation Teams) within the Metropolitan Police. She had always wanted to be a police officer, even as a kid, and she was a really good one. Not that she had ever told me much about her work, thankfully. Murders and such weren't things I particularly wanted to hear about and Erin was, and always has been, one of those people who keeps everything close to her chest.

Although, when one of our friends was toying with the idea of becoming a crime writer and had questioned Erin about her job, Erin had gone into quite a lot of detail at the dinner table. I'm not sure if it was her description of a rather grisly murder, or the prawn curry our host served at that dinner party, but a few people left the table saying they weren't feeling well.

Sometimes, when we were chatting, Erin made me feel as though I was sitting across the table from her in an interrogation room. Which was exactly how I was feeling at that moment, and I was half expecting her to ask me to sign a confession.

'I, Lucy Parkes, confess to the crime of doing something utterly stupid, by booking a break away for me and my boyfriend, Ted, knowing full well that the chances of him actually wanting to go away, are remote, to say the least.'

Of course, Erin was right. She always was.

Ted lived for his work and rarely, if ever, took time off. Not only was he on the partner-track at one of the largest accountancy firms in Kingston upon Thames, where we lived, he also did the accounts for several friends who ran small businesses but couldn't afford the hourly rates charged by the prestigious firm of SKM. The firm, like many other accountancy firms, used an abbreviation of the partnership name. But the partners of SKM had good reason. Sampson Krappe Moore didn't have quite the same ring. Even if it did make me and Erin giggle.

Ted did tell me, the day we met, that his work came first. It was one of the things that attracted me to him. In addition to his good-looks. I've always liked a man with a strong work ethic, and it was apparent from that very first night, that Ted had his future career path mapped out. But I foolishly thought that, as our relationship progressed, he would want to spend a little more time with me. If anything, we spend less time together now. Although, with the tax deadlines at the end of January, I understood that November, December, and January were busy months for him. But we'd been dating for a year last November, and after his promise on New Year's Eve, plus his suggestion that we should go away together, one of us had to book a getaway, so it might as well have been me. Especially as Ted hadn't mentioned it since.

But I'd booked this romantic break the day before, yet I still hadn't summoned up the nerve to tell Ted what I'd done.

And that wasn't just because I knew Ted was a workaholic. He also loved city-life — and the hamlet of Midwinter, where we were going for our romantic break, consisted of three cottages high up on Midwinter Ridge, and a farm in the valley below. Not exactly what one might call, buzzing.

However, the nearby town of Fairlight Bay, situated on the seaward side of Midwinter Ridge, had lots to offer.

And I should know. It's where I fell in love for the first time, ten years ago.

And where I made the biggest mistake of my life.

Which was why I had been having doubts about the romantic break I'd booked for me and Ted.

Why had I picked Midwinter? Out of all the places I could've chosen for a romantic week away – why there?

Was it because one of the results of the search I'd done for 'idyllic country cottage getaways in the UK,' listed Fairlight Bay as the place that offered everything I was looking for? Albeit on page five of those search results. Or was it because I had actively scrolled through each page of results until I had spotted the words, 'Fairlight Bay'?

Had I done it subconsciously?

I'd had a couple of glasses of wine at lunch yesterday. Had that impaired my thought process?

All I can say for certain is that the moment I saw the words, 'Fairlight Bay,' my heart gave a little leap, a warm flush spread over me, and a twinge of excitement swept through me.

I'd clicked on the link, scanned the list of

rental properties available for the dates I'd wanted, seen the cottage on Midwinter Ridge on the cute little lane with a babbling brook a mere stone's throw away, and typed in my credit card details within a matter of minutes.

And then came the downer.

The cottage might be perfect for me, but was it perfect for Ted? I loved the countryside; Ted – not so much. He preferred the city.

And was it wise to return to somewhere so close to Fairlight Bay after all these years? Would being in the place where I'd thought I'd met the love of my life, drag up all the pain and heartache I'd tried so hard to put behind me?

And what would I do if – by some quirk of fate – I bumped into *him*? The man who smashed my heart to smithereens.

I'd convinced myself that I was over him, but was that true? Would I ever get over him entirely? People say you never forget your first love. That was true for me. I hadn't forgotten him. I'd like to say that now, when I think of him, it's simply, happy memories, but that wouldn't be true. I told myself that I hardly remembered the man. That wasn't true either. I tried extremely hard *not* to remember him. Yet somehow, he still popped into my head every now and then.

However much I might have wished he wouldn't.

Sam Worth, the love of my life; the one who got away. The only man I'd ever truly loved. The one man who broke my heart.

Did he ever think of me? I doubted it. To Sam, it had merely been a holiday fling. He had made that abundantly clear.

'We'll be hundreds of miles apart,' he had said, on that last night we were together in Fairlight Bay. At that time, ten years ago last July, my family was about to move from Kingston upon Thames to Aberdeen, in Scotland, because my dad worked for a major oil company and his new position was based there. 'Long distance relationships rarely work,' Sam had added. 'And we're young. I want to travel the world. You're off to university in September. This has been fantastic. Something neither of us expected. But all good things must end, so they say. Don't you think?'

I remembered every word of that conversation; each one another knife in my heart. Yet there had been a hint of doubt in his voice at that moment and my foolish heart had held so much hope when I looked into his eyes and saw the lingering passion.

But that passion was mixed with confusion and fear and although he had held me in his arms, his body had been tense, and it was as if he was building a wall between us as he spoke. Brick by brick until, no matter what I might have said, I knew I couldn't break through. I had fallen in love. Sam had been in lust.

Yes, we were young. But at eighteen, we were adults. And yes, we would have been living hundreds of miles apart, but if Sam had asked me to stay in Fairlight Bay, I would've stayed. I would've done anything to be with him. But his mind was made up.

'Holiday flings happen,' he had said. 'Don't they? We'd be mad to think this was anything other than that. Wouldn't we?'

He was staring at me with a strange intensity, as if he were trying to convince us both, and then he looked away into the distance. No doubt thinking of all the girls he'd meet on his travels. I got the distinct impression that all he wanted to do was get away from me as quickly as possible. So, instead of telling him I loved him, I merely nodded and agreed.

'Yes,' I said simply, as my heart silently screamed during the ensuing silence.

'Yes? Okay. So we agree. Erm. If you're ever back in Fairlight Bay, come and see me,' he added, the words tumbling out as though he couldn't say them fast enough. 'And if I ever find myself in Aberdeen, I'll look you up. Or in Leeds, while you're at uni.' He swallowed hard and then he smiled the smile I'd fallen in love with the first time I saw it, except this time it seemed forced somehow. 'I'd better go.' He turned and walked away but after taking a few steps, he spun around and for a split second I thought he would run back to me and sweep me up in his strong arms. But he stood his ground. 'I wish things could be different,' he had said, his voice cracking as if he actually cared. 'You're ... you're special, Lucy. I won't forget you.'

'I'll never forget you, Sam,' I said. I desperately wanted to say that things could be different if we wanted them to be, but I couldn't seem to get the words out, and he abruptly turned and marched off, my heart breaking and tears rolling down my cheeks as I watched him walk away.

After the most incredible, magical, passionate, and romantic week of my life, we had gone our separate ways that night. And I hadn't seen him since.

Mum, Dad, and I had moved to Aberdeen, and in September I had gone to university in Leeds, but by the time I graduated, my parents had divorced and Mum had returned to Kingston upon Thames, a mere sixty miles or so away from Fairlight Bay.

While I was in Leeds, I had shared a house with three other girls and two guys.

During my second year there, I'd had a brief relationship with one of the guys, more in the hope that he might help me get over Sam than in the hope that anything would come of it. Needless to say, the relationship didn't last. Both my head and my heart constantly compared him to Sam. No one could compete with that memory.

When my heart could bear it, I'd looked Sam up on social media. He had a couple of accounts but he didn't seem to update them much. I'd been sorely tempted to get in touch, but I'd stopped myself. Just seeing his face – and that devastatingly gorgeous smile, brought back all the pain I'd felt that final night. Why would I put myself through that again? Only an idiot – or a masochist – would do that.

I'll admit, I did check his accounts for updates several times during the first few months, at least those that were open to the public, but he still didn't seem to be updating any of them, and as it hurt so much to look, I stopped looking. What was the point in wishing for something that could never be?

Sam Worth was just a holiday fling. He had told me so himself.

I had to accept that only one of us had fallen in love that week in Fairlight Bay.

And that had not been Sam.

Two

'You've booked a last-minute break? For us?'

Ted looked, and sounded, even more incredulous than Erin had when I eventually told him what I'd done. We were in my kitchen that evening and he almost spilt his bottle of beer, but he managed to upright it in time, before a drop plopped onto my tiled floor.

I'd made pizza. Well, I'd taken it out of the fridge, and its packaging, and stuck it in the oven for the required twelve minutes, while Ted had opened a beer for himself, and poured me another large glass of red wine from the bottle I'd opened earlier. It was my third of the evening, because I'd needed a glass or two before he arrived, for courage.

I was going to wait until after we'd eaten to tell him, but whilst dating Ted, experience had taught me that it was better not to put things off. His phone might ring and he might dash off to do something work-related, and then I wouldn't get a chance because he'd say we'd have to discuss it another time. But if I told him something straight away, he might still dash off, but he'd come back later to finish our conversation, or at least, call me to do so. That's what I'd learnt over the last year and a bit.

So, after we had asked one another if we'd had a good day, and I'd told him I'd met up with Erin before she went on her shift, and he'd told me he'd spent most of his day in client meetings and how busy his had been, I had broached the subject.

'A last-minute *romantic* break,' I clarified, and he gave me an even stranger look. 'You said we should go away,' I reminded him. 'And you said February was a good time after the January rush.'

I worked with my mum, running a bridal shop in the Bentall Shopping Centre in Kingston upon Thames, along with an online extension of that business, so I could take time off whenever I wanted, within reason. Ted had told me at the new year that as he was owed so much holiday, having rarely taken any time off, he could also have a few days off, or a week, at short notice. But perhaps he had meant more notice than just one day.

He took a long swig from his bottle, and I gulped more wine, and then he looked at me, his brows knit tightly together.

'I did say that. That's true. But that was before I knew you were terrified of flying. I was thinking of somewhere hot when I said that.'

I had only told Ted on New Year's Eve that, despite being the grand old age of twenty-eight, I had never been on a plane. Just the thought of it made my stomach churn, my heart thump, and my head spin. He had been astonished and had asked why I hadn't told him about my fear before, as though I'd kept some deep dark secret from him and that I was a mass murderer or something equally awful. But the subject had simply never come up. We hadn't discussed holidays, or places we'd been – or hadn't been, until that night.

I suppose, on some level, I might have intentionally kept it from him. People always looked at me like I was a bit mad or something, when I mentioned my phobia, so over the years, I never brought it up unless someone actually asked. And Ted hadn't asked. It was only when he'd suggested on New Year's Eve that we should go away together to somewhere like Tenerife, or the Caribbean, that I said we'd have to go by ship.

And just like everyone else had in the past, Ted had looked at me as if I were some sort of Alien being.

Since that night, things had slightly changed between us. Erin told me I was imagining it at first, but I knew I wasn't. Which was one of the reasons I'd booked the romantic break for Ted and me. I wanted things to go back to the way they were on New Year's Eve. Before I'd told him I would never get on a plane.

'I know,' I said. 'But this'll be fun. We'll sleep late, take leisurely lunches, long walks in the bracing, sea air–'

'Long walks?' he interjected, his brows raised as I was trying to think of other things we could do. 'It's done nothing but rain for the last few weeks. Not really holiday weather, is it? February in the UK isn't quite so appealing.'

'That depends.' I hoped my smile was seductive. 'A cosy cottage with a roaring log fire, just you and me, and the rain pounding against the windows.' I leant forward and walked my fingertips up the front of his pristine white shirt, making sure each finger landed on a button. 'That sounds very appealing to me.'

Ted's body reacted to my touch and he plonked his beer bottle on the counter and reached out for me. A sudden crash of thunder made us both jump.

And then an image popped into my mind's eye as rain lashed against my kitchen window. But it wasn't of me and Ted.

It was of me and Sam, on a hot and humid July night, kissing on the beach in Fairlight Bay, waves gently lapping at our bare feet, our toes half buried in the wet sand, as thunder rumbled around us. And then, with one almighty crash, the clouds burst, sending torrents of rain down on us. I could almost hear my shriek of surprise, and Sam's deep, melodic laugh as he took my hand and we ran for cover, taking shelter in the beach hut his family owned.

We had only met that day and yet I felt as if I'd known him all my life. Making love with him that night not only seemed the most natural thing in the world to do, it felt like my life depended on it. As if I couldn't breathe without him kissing me, as if my heart might stop if it didn't beat in rhythm with his, as if my body would crumble without his arms around me.

'Are you sure?' Sam had moaned softly, aware that this was the first time for me, after we had torn off each other's clothes.

'Yes,' I had gasped, desperate for his touch. 'Oh yes.'

I had never been more certain of anything in my life.

'Lucy?'

Ted's voice brought me back to the reality of my kitchen but I couldn't stop the strangled sigh from escaping at the loss of that memory.

'Sorry,' I said. 'I was ... watching the rain.'

He gave me a doubtful look, having stepped away from me after the boom of thunder, instead of pulling me in for a kiss. The storm must've distracted him too.

'Hmm. Yes. Well. That sort of proves my point, doesn't it? Walks in the rain seem more likely than anything. And that doesn't sound like fun to me.'

'Well I'm sorry,' I snapped, partly cross with myself for being so stupid as to make a booking without checking with him first, and partly cross at him for not seeming to be keen to spend time away with me in a cosy, country cottage. 'I thought us spending seven days together would be fun. And romantic. And, oh silly me, I assumed you'd jump at the chance of having seven nights of sex without needing to get up early for work every morning.'

I glowered at Ted but he met my angry stare with silence, and then the alarm I'd set for the oven timer, beeped.

'I suppose we should eat,' Ted eventually said.

'Yes,' I agreed, turning off the alarm. 'We should eat.'

Three

'Have you paid a deposit?' Ted asked, a couple of hours later when we'd finally settled on the sofa together, after I'd loaded the dishwasher, cleaned the kitchen, and put the rubbish out, while he'd answered three phone calls and spent over an hour doing some work on his laptop for "an important client". Ted had another beer and I had yet another glass of wine, finishing the bottle. 'You'll get a refund, won't you? When you cancel.'

We had eaten in silence until Ted had eventually asked for more details of the cottage in Midwinter, but it had quickly become clear that he had no intention of going and that anything I might have said to try to persuade him would have been futile, so I hadn't tried.

'Erm.' I clicked on the TV remote and an episode of *Love Island All Stars* popped up on the screen. I immediately changed channels. I didn't need the competition. My body wasn't bad, but I tried to keep it covered as much as possible. Especially in the winter months when it was more the colour of porridge than sun-kissed bronze. Neither of us were football fans, but an *FA Cup Final* was preferable, in my opinion at least, to the other offerings. I hadn't renewed my subscriptions to any of the streaming services because one of my new year resolutions had been to watch less TV. 'I had to pay the full amount. It was a last-minute booking. And it's Valentine's Day next Friday, so no.'

His head shot round so that he could look at me. 'You won't get a refund?'

'Not if I cancel. No.' I stared at the TV as one of the footballers rolled around on the wet grass, hugging his right knee.

Ted shifted his position and his torso was now facing me, 'What do you mean, "not if I cancel"? We discussed it. I can't just swan off for a week without giving my firm proper notice.'

I turned my head to meet his eyes. 'And yet you said during supper that if I changed it to somewhere hot, you'd be happy to help me "get over my little problem with flying." And that you could email Babs in HR and tell her, and it'd probably be fine.'

'No, I...' He lowered his gaze and shook his head before looking at me once more.

'Okay. I did say that. But come on, Lucy. You know I'm not particularly into the countryside. And long walks don't really do it for me. Especially not in the rain. I'm sure you'll be able to get a refund. Even if it's only a partial one.'

'What if I don't want to? Cancel, I mean.'

His mouth opened and then closed and his brows knit together before he spoke.

'Why wouldn't you want to cancel? I know you probably meant it as a pleasant surprise, but as I said earlier, you should've discussed it with me before you booked. I don't want to spend a week in a cottage in the middle of nowhere. Cancel, and we'll do something special on Valentine's Day. I'll take the day off and we'll spend it together.' He looked away from me and glanced at the TV. A roar had gone up among the crowd and the footballers were now all hugging one another after one of them had scored a goal. 'Erm. As it happens, I've just been told about a networking event next weekend and ... I think perhaps I should go to that. That was one of the calls I got tonight.'

I didn't ask for details and Ted didn't immediately offer any, but he was right. I should've discussed it with him first, before I'd booked our week away. I don't know why I hadn't.

And yet, perhaps I did know why.

Something had definitely changed between us since New Year's Eve. Not by a huge amount, but by enough for me to know there had been a change. And then Mum had asked me a couple of weeks ago if everything was going okay between me and Ted, so even she had noticed. Erin said I was imagining it at first but last week, on one of our regular, girls' nights out, she agreed with me.

'Ted's never been overly effusive on the romance front,' Erin had said, 'But I agree it's odd that he hasn't mentioned doing something on Valentine's Day. Last year he told you three weeks before that he was planning a surprise treat for you. I remember, because I said that as he'd told you he was planning a surprise, it wasn't a genuine surprise. And you said it was a surprise, because you didn't know what the actual treat was. And then it turned out to be dinner in the restaurant at the pub where you'd met.'

'Yes. And you sarcastically said that you'd never heard of anything so romantic.'

Erin had laughed. 'It was hardly imaginative, was it? Dinner in a pub restaurant. I said it then and I'll say it again now. Surely he could've come up with something better than that?'

'At least he made an effort. This year, he hasn't said a word.'

'Perhaps this year he's actually keeping his epic romantic gesture a secret.'

'Do you think so?' I had brightened at that prospect.

'No,' Erin had unceremoniously replied. 'I think he's been so focussed on his work that he's forgotten about it entirely. And last year, I remember you saying how excited you were about Valentine's Day. This year you've hardly mentioned it.'

That conversation had made me realise that the change in my relationship with Ted wasn't just down to him; I had cooled off too.

When I'd told Mum about it at work the following day, she had said that all relationships go through this as couples settled into their own routines.

I didn't want a routine. And I didn't want to settle.

Yes, I wanted to get married, have kids, and pets, and everything else that falling deeply in love usually led to, but settle into a routine? No thank you. I wanted to be with someone who made my heart soar, my mind fizz with excitement, and my body burn with desire, each and every day. I wanted the sort of love I'd be willing to do anything for.

Was that the stuff of fairytales?

Perhaps it was.

But that was how Sam had made me feel.

Okay, that had been ten years ago, and I

was only eighteen at the time. But I was only twenty-eight now, and I wanted those things. I had always wanted those things.

That was why I had booked a romantic getaway for me and Ted to that cottage in Midwinter.

After one year and a few months together, Ted and I were drifting apart. I could feel it. He hadn't booked anything for Valentine's Day. I hadn't been certain of that, but I somehow knew he hadn't. He had confirmed that tonight when he'd said that if I cancelled, we could go out for dinner on Valentine's Day. He hadn't said that he had already booked something.

And I hadn't been excited about Valentine's Day this year either. If we were going to save our relationship, one of us had to do something to rekindle that spark.

I was hoping that being so close to Fairlight Bay, the place where I'd experienced the best week of my life, not to mention, the best sex of my life, might reignite something in me. And hopefully ignite something in Ted.

How stupid of me.

I had wanted to spend a week with Ted in a cosy, country cottage in Midwinter in the hope that some of the magic I'd felt in Fairlight Bay ten years ago, might waft over us, and make us fall in love. Deeply, madly, and passionately in love.

Because we weren't.

We liked each other a lot, but love?

Neither of us had said those three little words, and the chances of us ever saying them were getting less each day.

This evening, I had also realised that I wanted to get away from the hustle and bustle of Kingston upon Thames. Away from the bridal shop, and the online side of the business that I helped my mum run, where every bride-to-be gushed about her upcoming marriage with the love of her life. The man of her dreams. Her one true love. Away from the constant reminder that, the way things were going, it would probably never be me. Because the only man I had ever truly loved, had broken my heart ten years ago, and no one since had made me feel the way that he had.

When I'd met Ted, I had thought he might come close, but the longer we dated, the more it seemed unlikely. I'd booked this romantic break in a sort of last-ditch attempt to see if we could make a go of it. But in doing so, the only thing I would have possibly achieved was the thing I was determined not to: I would be settling.

I wanted to be in love. Deeply in love as I once was. All those years ago. Would I ever feel that way again? Why wasn't I lucky with love?

Perhaps the problem wasn't with the men I dated. Perhaps the problem was with me. I still hadn't got over Sam, even after all these years, I was clinging to the past.

So I was going to spend a week in a cosy, country cottage in Midwinter and try to sort myself out. Whether Ted came with me or not. And I wanted to go back to Fairlight Bay and to try to exorcise those ghosts. The ghosts of a long-lost love.

Was I being overly dramatic? Probably.

But after I'd had that little flashback earlier, I couldn't get Sam out of my mind. And I had to get him out. Once and for all. I had to move on from my past if I was ever going to have the future I wanted.

Four

Ted, it transpired, had been making plans of his own. Plans that didn't include me. It wasn't merely his unwillingness to spend a week in a cottage in the middle of nowhere that had made him decline to come with me to Midwinter – although at first it had been that. But, as he'd briefly mentioned, one of the calls he had taken that evening, after we'd eaten, had been from a friend of his. This friend had organised a last-minute break of his own. A four-day break to a golf resort in Vilamoura in the Algarve region of Portugal the following weekend. A work-related jolly that Ted had called, a Networking Event.

Ted had apparently told his friend that he couldn't go, but it was obvious he wanted to. Portugal might not be hot in February but the weather would undoubtedly be better than it would be in the UK. When I had said that I wasn't going to cancel my booking to Midwinter, whether Ted came with me or not, Ted had decided he would rather go to

Vilamoura. He'd be flying out in the early evening on Friday the fourteenth, and returning the following Tuesday. And if I spent the entire week in Midwinter, it would mean we wouldn't see one another on Valentine's Day.

Which was fair enough. I had no grounds for complaint. I'd booked a week away without checking with him. I couldn't blame him for preferring Vilamoura to Midwinter.

But it wasn't as simple as that.

After consuming an entire bottle of wine, I would normally sleep through the night, awaking around seven as usual, but once Ted and I had made love – which had also been different somehow, I woke to find Ted dressing. Assuming it was morning, I raised my head. But the shaft of light streaming through the gap between the curtains and spotlighting Ted as though he were on stage, was moonlight, not daylight. I glanced at the clock beside my bed on which the digital display read two a.m.

'You're leaving?' I asked, not quite sure what was going on as I switched on my bedside lamp.

Ted was visibly startled. He looked like a rabbit caught in headlights.

'Oh. Erm. Yes. I didn't mean to wake you. Sorry.'

I glanced at the clock again, unable to

fathom what was happening.

'But it's two a.m. Why are you leaving at this time of night? Sorry. Morning.'

He grimaced and ran a hand over his close-cropped fair hair, his blue eyes darting from left to right as though he were searching for an appropriate answer. Then he stepped into his trousers, tucked in his shirt, and pulled up the zip.

'Erm. The thing is, Lucy. This isn't really working.'

Still sleep addled, I asked, 'What isn't? Everything seemed to be working fine last night.'

'I meant us, Lucy. We're not working.'

'Us? Our relationship you mean? And you decided this sometime between the hours of midnight, after we'd had sex, and now, at two a.m.?'

He coughed to clear his throat as he grabbed his tie from the back of my dressing table chair, and folded it up before pushing it into his trouser pocket.

'I couldn't sleep. So yes. I've been thinking about it for the past two hours. I really like you, Lucy. You know I do. But something's been different for the last few weeks. It feels as if ... we're drifting along but not going anywhere. And then there's this thing of yours about planes. I'm not sure what to do with that.'

'Planes? Oh, my fear of flying, you mean. Why's that suddenly a problem?' I raised myself onto my elbows and glared at him. 'We've been dating for well over a year and it hasn't been an issue until now.'

'Let's not make this any more difficult than it needs to be.' He picked up his jacket and slung it on. 'It's an issue because you kept it from me. I did wonder why you and Erin went down to Bournemouth for a week last summer and not abroad, but when me and my mates flew off to Barcelona for Jerry's stag weekend, you never said you were afraid to fly. When you told me about it at the new year, I was shocked. And now with this cottage break thing, it got me thinking. I don't want to spend my holidays in the UK. I want to go abroad.'

'I want to go abroad too. But via the Channel tunnel, or by ferry, or on a cruise ship, not by plane.'

He shrugged. 'Yeah well. Good luck with that. Sorry. That sounded mean. I don't want to fall out with you, because I meant it when I said I really like you. But ... I think we want different things. For example, you want to rent a country cottage and take long walks by the sea and listen to the rain. I want to stay in a five-star hotel, with a heated pool, and a golf course. And I only realised that tonight. As weird as that seems.'

I couldn't argue with that. I only realised tonight that I'd booked that break to try to save our relationship, even though I knew Ted wasn't a fan of the countryside.

'It's not weird.' I shook my head and sighed loudly. 'You're right. Things have been different between us since New Year's Eve. I've felt it too. But were you intending to simply skulk off into the night without telling me?'

'No.' He was clearly offended by that allegation. 'I just decided that if I didn't go now, I might not want to go. I was going to leave you a note in the kitchen.'

'Oh really.' That was almost as bad. 'And what was this note going to say?'

He shrugged once again. 'That I had to go but that I'd call you.'

'Oh I see. Not, "Hey. It's over. See you around." Or something like that?'

'No. I just didn't want any drama, that's all. And I didn't want to spoil your week away. I thought I'd leave it vague and then, once you get back from ... wherever that place was, and I get back from Portugal, we'd meet up and ... break up then. Probably. Unless I felt ... erm. Differently by then.'

'Ah. Keeping your options open. Very wise. But this isn't just about how you feel, Ted. This is also about me. Why couldn't we have simply had a conversation about it over breakfast?'

He smiled sheepishly. 'I suppose that would've been the right thing to do. But I was feeling guilty. And as I said, I didn't want any drama. Sorry, Lucy. I should've thought about your feelings, not just mine.'

I could see he was telling the truth and although this wasn't how I would've ended our relationship, there was no point in prolonging the inevitable.

'That's okay, Ted. I understand. This might be because I'm still half asleep, but it's fine. You go. And don't worry about calling me.'

It was as if the executioner had stayed his axe, and Ted's sigh of relief was audible.

'Thanks for understanding. Have fun in...' He screwed up his eyes.

'Midwinter. Thanks, Ted. Have a good time in Vilamoura. I hope you don't get rain.'

He grinned at me and then dashed over to my side of the bed, bending down to plonk a kiss on the top of my head.

'It's been great, Lucy.' He winked. 'See you around.'

I gave him a small smile. 'Yeah. Whatever. Please make sure the front door is locked behind you. I'm going back to sleep.'

I turned off the light and snuggled down beneath my duvet, keeping my eyes open until I heard the front door click shut.

But when I closed my eyes, I couldn't get back to sleep. I had known things weren't going that well between us over the last few weeks, but I hadn't wanted to end our relationship. I had been trying to save it.

Ted was right though. It was probably for the best.

I wasn't sure how I felt.

Certainly not heartbroken. I had only experienced that once.

A little sad, perhaps.

I puffed out a long sigh as it dawned on me that, once again, I had been unlucky in love. And once again, I was single.

Would I ever find someone who truly loved me? And someone I truly loved in return.

Five

I had a bit of a hangover the next day, and was also tired from a lack of sleep, so when Mum told me I could have the afternoon off, I jumped at the chance. I had told her about Ted and me splitting up and although she said she was sorry, she hadn't seemed that surprised.

'You'll know when you meet the right one, my darling,' she said, turning the sign on the shop door to say 'closed'. We shut the bridal shop for half an hour each day from twelve-thirty till one, because Mum believed a work-life balance was important. And yet she always checked the online orders while eating her sandwich, or her salad, or whatever she was having for lunch that day. 'Ted obviously wasn't Mr Right.'

I followed her into one of the back rooms where we had a kitchenette, a small circular table and two chairs, plus a two-seater sofa.

'Did you think Dad was the right one?' I asked, after a moment or two as I filled the

35

kettle to make tea.

She shrugged and smiled, taking her tuna sandwich from the fridge, and placing it on a plate on the table.

'I was only fourteen when I met him and all I could think about was how handsome he was. He looked like an angel with his golden blond hair and green eyes. When we married, I wasn't grown up enough at sixteen to realise that he was the type of man who would find marriage and things like mortgages and other responsibilities, boring. He tried his best, but I'm surprised we stayed together for as long as we did after you left for uni. He only did that for you.'

I loved my dad, and I knew he loved me, but it had taken a while for me to forgive him for telling Mum he wanted a divorce. Since they divorced, he'd had several girlfriends but no one serious. Mum on the other hand, had remarried. My stepdad was a lovely man named Chris.

'And Chris?' I queried.

Mum's smile said it all. 'I knew from the moment he touched my hand.' I'd heard the story of how they met, many times, but I never tired of hearing it. 'We were in Sainsbury's and we both reached up for a jar of olives that were on the top shelf. I couldn't quite reach, so, like the gentleman he is, Chris handed me a jar, and his fingers brushed mine. It was like a bolt of electricity and we just stood and stared at one another. Until someone else wanted to get to the olives. We smiled at each other and then I turned and walked away, but he came after me and asked if he could buy me a coffee. It was only later that he realised he hadn't got a jar of olives for himself. So yes. I knew he was Mr Right from that very first moment.'

That's exactly how I'd felt when I'd met Sam. And I'd experienced a similar bolt of electricity the first time Sam's hand had brushed against my skin. But I'd never told Mum that.

Even after all these years, I hadn't told her how much I'd loved Sam. She knew I'd met him on the very first day of that holiday, ten years before, of course, and that we were seeing one another. Sam and I had spent almost every moment of that week together so someone would have had to be blind not to know that.

She'd asked me one evening if I was "being careful" and told me that, if I wanted to talk to her about anything, anything at all, I could. But the only person I told was Erin. I'd phoned or texted or video-called her every day.

And when Sam broke my heart, the day we left Fairlight Bay, I hadn't told Mum. I'd said I'd caught a cold, which was why my eyes were running, and then I'd spent most of the following week in my room. Erin had visited me every day and hugged me while I'd cried. Moving so far away from Erin, when Mum, Dad, and I went to Aberdeen, had been almost as devastating. Except I still spoke to Erin every day. I never spoke to Sam again.

'Is this anything to do with that boy?' Mum asked me once or twice.

'Him? Oh no. That was just a holiday fling.' It tore my heart to shreds just to repeat Sam's words, but Mum had seemed convinced.

I'm not sure why I was so reluctant to tell Mum how I felt. Perhaps, because I knew she had problems of her own. I'd heard my parents arguing a few times over the years, but after that holiday, when we moved to Aberdeen, the rows grew more frequent. Mum didn't really want to leave Kingston upon Thames, but, as she told me after they'd divorced, she had thought that moving there with Dad might be the only way to save their marriage. Obviously, that hadn't worked.

I'd left for uni in Leeds a few weeks later, so I was able to keep my heartbreak to myself. Well, myself and Erin. I'm not sure how I would've coped without all those long chats with my best friend.

'Do you regret marrying Dad?' I asked Mum now.

Her shocked expression was its own reply. 'Never. If I hadn't married him, I wouldn't have had you. And you're the best thing that's ever happened to me, my darling.'

I smiled at her. 'Apart from meeting Chris.'

She grinned and winked. 'He comes a close second.'

I handed her a cup of tea and sat on the chair opposite with my own cup.

'Where's your lunch?' she asked as she bit into her tuna sandwich.

I shrugged. 'I forgot it this morning. But I'm not hungry.'

'You've got to eat, Lucy. Why don't you nip out and get something? No wait. I've got a better idea. Take the afternoon off. I know you won't have packed yet. And you're leaving tomorrow, aren't you?'

'You're correct on both counts?' I grinned. 'But are you sure? I'll be away for a week and I didn't give you much notice. Don't you want me to stay and help you today?'

'We're not rushed off our feet in the shop, are we? And Chris will help me with all the online orders, so there's no need for you to worry about those. No. You go, my darling. And have a wonderful time.'

I took a few gulps of my tea and then

beamed at her as I got to my feet.

'Well if you're sure. Thanks, Mum. You're the best.' I dashed to the sink, washed up my cup, and left it to drain on the plastic drip tray on the counter. 'You can call me if you need anything. You know that, don't you?'

Mum nodded and smiled. 'And the same goes for you. Call me if you want to chat.'

I kissed her on the cheek, grabbed my raincoat from the rack and headed towards the door. It had rained for most of the week and my faux fur jacket had got drenched the day before.

'I will, Mum. Bye. Hope you have a good week.'

'And you, my darling. Oh. And if you bump into that handsome young man, say hello from me.'

I stopped in my tracks and spun round, my voice cracking as I spoke.

'Which handsome young man?'

'Sam,' she said, her gaze fixed on the last piece of her sandwich. 'That was his name, wasn't it?'

I swallowed the lump in my throat, and squeaked, 'Sam?' I coughed and took a quick breath to compose myself. 'Oh. The holiday fling, you mean. I'm not sure I'd even recognise him. Bye. Love you.'

I raced out of the room, and the shop,

before either of us could say anything more.

Had Mum known all these years, how I'd felt about Sam?

'Of course she has,' Erin said, when I called and told her about the conversation, and that I'd got the afternoon off.

I'd already called her first thing that morning to tell her Ted and I had broken up. She'd listened intently, and then offered to pop round that evening with a takeaway and some wine. I'd told her I couldn't drink because I'd be driving down to Midwinter the following day, to which she had replied, 'That's fine. More wine for me.'

'Are you still coming round this evening?' I checked.

'Absolutely. I might be a little late though. We're a bit busy at the moment.'

'Those pesky criminals,' I joked. 'Sorry. I know murder isn't funny. I'm in a strange mood.'

'Don't worry about it. Laughter helps to keep us sane. It's a crazy world out there. See you around seven.'

Six

When Ted had told me he wouldn't be joining me on the break I'd booked in Midwinter, I was disappointed, but not that bothered. A week by myself in a cottage in the countryside, close enough to a town that I wouldn't feel isolated, wouldn't be that bad. It might give me the opportunity to sort myself out and decide what I wanted. It might even help me think of new ways to improve my relationship with Ted. Or so I had convinced myself.

But after our subsequent break up, what I was facing was a week alone. And somehow that was different. A far more daunting prospect. Nonetheless, I had been determined to go. Partly because, as a last-minute booking, there would not be a refund, and partly because ... well, because I couldn't stop thinking about Sam.

I had no idea if he still lived in Fairlight Bay. No clue as to whether or not he had a girlfriend – or a wife. I hadn't looked at his social media for years, having realised that to do so was a self-inflicted wound. And self-harm was something I would avoid at all cost.

Erin, on the other hand, decided we should look him up, which was the first thing she said when she arrived at my door, takeaway in one hand, wine bottle in the other.

'Now that you and Ted are over, let's see if Sam is available. We'll start with social media, but if that doesn't give us any answers, I could call a colleague in the Fairlight Bay force if you like. Strictly speaking, we're not supposed to use any information, systems, or services, for personal purposes, but lots of officers do, and it would only be a friendly chat.'

'Erin! No. I would hate it if someone did that to me. Social media's a different thing. I'm okay with searching that because it's open to the public. Although I'm not sure if I want to.'

She tutted and rolled her eyes. 'We both know that's a lie.'

She was right, of course, as always, and once we'd eaten, we had settled ourselves on the sofa, with my laptop open on the coffee table in front of us.

'I suppose it would be good to see what he looks like now,' I said. 'Just in case I bump into him somewhere and I don't recognise him.'

Erin laughed at that. 'Yeah. Because he'll have changed so much in ten years.'

'He might have. Ten years is a long time.'

'You look the same as you did ten years ago. A couple of wrinkles here and there but other than that.' She raised her arms to defend herself from the cushion I'd hit her with.

'Watch it,' I warned.

She pointed her forefinger back at herself. 'Police officer here. You're the one who should watch it. Assaulting an officer is a criminal offence.'

I gave her a nudge and she nudged me back and then we grinned at one another.

'Okay. Let's do this,' I said, picking up my glass and taking a long gulp of my orange juice before typing Sam's full name into the search bar.

Erin knocked back half of her glass of wine and made a satisfied, 'Ahhh' sound.

'Nectar of the gods,' she said. 'Wow. Talking of gods, is that him? I'd forgotten he looked that good.'

We exchanged glances and then both leant forward and peered at the screen.

'So had I,' I said, unable to keep the wistful tone from my voice. It had been several years since I'd seen his photo.

'Have you noticed, he's the opposite of Ted?' Erin pointed out.

'Uh-huh,' I agreed, as heat rushed through my body.

How could just a photo of the man have this much of an effect on me?

'And not merely in looks,' I eventually added. 'Unless he's changed. Ted's a workaholic and loves his job. Sam believed work was a necessary evil. Although he was only nineteen when we ... when I knew him, so maybe that's different now.'

They were definitely opposites.

Ted had close-cropped fair hair, blue eyes and was well-groomed. He liked the things that money could buy.

Sam had – and judging from the photos we were looking at, still had – wild, dark hair, dark eyes, tanned skin, and now a hint of stubble on his firm jaw. When we had spent that week together, Sam had lived in jeans and T-shirts, or shorts during the long, hot days of July. And money meant little to him in those days. Happiness and having fun were all that mattered.

Ted wasn't overly romantic. Sam had been the most romantic man I'd ever met.

Ted was good in bed. Sam had been amazing. But I was eighteen at the time and Sam was the first man I'd had sex with, so maybe I remembered it as better than it was.

All I could say for sure was that I'd compared every man I'd dated since then, with Sam, and they'd all been wanting in one way or another.

Ted was the longest relationship I'd had, so he must have been doing something right. Until it had all gone wrong.

'Well,' Erin said, raising her glass and clinking it with mine. 'Here's to you finding out whether or not Sam has changed.' She grinned. 'And maybe to you taking up where the two of you left off.'

Just the thought of that made me nearly spill my orange juice.

Even now, I could remember what it felt like to be in Sam's arms. What would I give to be in them again?

But if I did get the chance, would I take it? He had broken my heart once, could I afford to take the risk that he might do so for a second time?

It had been ten years, and I still wasn't over him completely. Did I really want to feel like this for another ten years?

Seven

I'm not sure I believed in good omens, or magic (although that week with Sam ten years ago was definitely magical) or even in Destiny, but it was as if the stars were aligned as I packed up my car the next morning and headed towards Fairlight Bay and the tiny hamlet of Midwinter.

The rain we'd had all week had stopped and the sky was the bluest of blues without so much as a puff of cloud in sight. The sun, which had been noticeably absent for some time, was not only shining brightly, it was warmer than it should have been for the time of year. It might've been the start of the second week in February, but the air was spring-like and the cold winds of the previous week had blown themselves out. I even had my window open for part of the journey.

I had left my home at ten having calculated that the latest I'd arrive was twelve, even if I hit traffic. It was eleven thirty-five when I saw the 'Welcome to Fairlight Bay' sign beside the road.

I had printed out the directions, having been advised that as Midwinter was so small, not all navigation systems seemed able to find it, and most gave directions to Midwinter Farm which was in the valley below on the leeward side of Midwinter Ridge. There were three cottages high up on Midwinter Ridge, one of which was the one I'd booked, and there was only one lane that led to the cottages. Midwinter Lane was absent from several road maps so I wasn't going to take any chances.

I arrived at a junction with three signposts and three roads ahead. One pointed to Fairlight Bay, one to Midwinter Farm, and the third to Midwinter Ridge. I was to take the third and then, after about half a mile I would see a small sign for Midwinter Lane. If I missed that, I would end up skirting the back of the town of Fairlight Bay.

As I seemed to be the only vehicle on this road, or should I say lane, which was what this one was, I drove slowly. Even so, I nearly missed the sign and had to brake hard and reverse back a little to turn into Midwinter Lane. Thank goodness it wasn't dark or raining. I'd never have spotted that sign.

I remember Sam telling me all those

years ago, that Midwinter Ridge was the group of hills that rose behind Fairlight Bay, sheltering it from the worst of the winter winds from the North, and that they were also known as the fire hills. This was because the wild gorse bushes that grew on the seaward side were covered in a blanket of yellow-gold blooms in the spring, giving the appearance of being on fire. It was too early yet to see this display but within a few weeks the hills would be transformed.

Sam had also told me that Midwinter Ridge could be reached by foot from almost anywhere along both the seaward and the leeward side of the hills, but I'd now discovered that the only way to reach the three cottages that stood on the ridge, by car, or any other vehicle, was via Midwinter Lane.

The first part of the lane was fine, but I could see the rest of it was far too narrow for cars and was unadopted. It was made up of sandstone, rocks, and rubble with the odd smattering of tarmac dotted here and there and I was more than a little relieved that I didn't have to drive on that. I took the turn off for the allocated car parking area which I had been told was opposite the cottages. This was clearly a much more recent addition and it had been tarmacked, I was pleased to see.

I pulled up beside three other vehicles, one of which was a van and bore a sign with

Alec Richman, plumbing and heating engineer, on the side. I hoped he wasn't dealing with a heating or plumbing problem in the cottage I was renting. But then I recalled being told that the boyfriend of the woman who lived in Middle Cottage, the centre of the row of three, was a plumber, so that was a relief. I couldn't recall the woman's name though.

I got out of my car and took in the vista before me. But it was chilly up here, so I opened the rear door and grabbed my faux fur jacket, the scarf that Erin had bought me for Christmas, and my black leather gloves from the back seat, and put them on to keep out the cold. Then I soaked up the view once more.

The hills of Midwinter Ridge were as impressive as I remembered, and the rooftops and buildings in Fairlight Bay below, glowed in the morning sunshine. The sea was a greeny-blue and it sparkled as if Neptune had cast a net of flashing fairy lights across the glass-like water.

My mind drifted and I wondered if Sam was somewhere down there in Fairlight Bay, and if so, what he might be doing, but I quickly pulled myself together. I wasn't here to think about Sam Worth.

I turned my back on the town and looked at the cottages. All three were bathed in sunshine and all three looked equally welcoming. They were also remarkably similar, each one having a tiled roof with two stubby chimneys either end, and three casement windows built in. The ground floors of each cottage had two larger casement windows either side of a central front door, framed by a stone pediment, one of which had been painted a fawn colour to match the façade. That one had a brown front door and when I spotted the red post box by the garden fence, I realised it was Far Cottage, the one in which I would be staying. The cottage next door was painted a bright fuchsia with a lime green front door, and the third was a soft grey with a black front door, each cottage garden separated by low hedges and edged with wooden rail fences.

Midwinter Brook separated the cottages from the car park and an old wooden footbridge stood over the babbling brook. The water looked cold and yet beautiful as it danced over the rocks, and pulled at the reeds running along the edges. A Canada Goose attempted a landing and then thought better of it, its massive wings flapping so close to me that I could feel the breeze on my face, as it flew up into the clear blue sky, before turning to give it a second try.

The brook ran close by the row of cottages and I was aware that it was a tributary of Midwinter River which was about two miles away. The river cascaded down one side of Midwinter Ridge, then flowed past Midwinter Farm, before it curved back around the foot of the hills and made its way through Fairlight Glen and then skirted the town on its way to the sea.

I remembered Fairlight Glen so well. It was a beautiful area of woodland and shrubs in which Sam and I had ... No. I must not think about Sam. And definitely not about what we had done in Fairlight Glen.

I shook off that memory as fast as I could, and studied the cottages. I had no idea who had built them, or why whomever it was, had chosen such a high and exposed place to do so, away from the town, and yet visible from almost anywhere in Fairlight Bay, but I remembered Sam telling me they had been farm cottages originally, dating back to the Middle Ages. They were rebuilt in the early 1800s to replace the former, much smaller dwellings.

All the land for miles around had once been part of the ancient, Midwinter Farm, but most of it had been sold off. Looking at the map and online information, the farm was little more than a smallholding now, consisting of a few fields of sheep and cows, some chickens and ducks, and a rather grand Elizabethan Farmhouse that had also replaced the original.

I got my bags from the car and walked over the footbridge. I'd expected it to be rickety as it looked rather old, but it didn't even creak as I made my way across and headed towards my home for the next seven days.

Far Cottage. Not an especially appealing name, but the online photos I had seen of the interior, made it look warm, welcoming, and romantic. It could also hold its own against any other property in one of those home design magazines.

The owner had told me via email that she and her partner, who was a property developer, had recently refurbished the entire cottage. So recently in fact that she joked that the paint might still be wet. At least I hoped she had been joking. It was apparent from the photos that they had spared no expense, although she hadn't said so.

But she had added, during a subsequent phone conversation, that she had lived there herself until a few days before Christmas, when she had moved into her partner's cottage, just two doors away.

'So if you need anything, you don't have far to come to ask me,' she had said.

Her name was Adele and her partner's name was Marcus. She clearly liked to talk because she also told me that it had been her partner's idea for her to rent her cottage out and that I would be the first person to occupy it.

'Wow,' I had said, somewhat surprised. 'I hope I don't put you off doing so again.'

I realised too late that I shouldn't have joked about that, but she merely laughed.

'Oh no,' she informed me. 'I need the money. I lost my job as head baker and pastry chef at a swanky hotel a few years ago and now I work as a waitress at Fairlight Bakes Café, in Fairlight Bay. The money isn't as good as I was used to but the owners are lovely. Marcus has offered to help me out, but I want to pay my own way. Do you have a boyfriend?'

'Yes,' I had said, as I was dating Ted when I'd booked. I wasn't sure if I was supposed to tell her that it would only be me after we had split up, but she'd find out soon enough.

'You'll have seen there are three cottages here on Midwinter Lane,' Adele had continued. 'Obviously, Far Cottage is where you'll be staying, and Marcus and I live in End Cottage. Our friend, Noelle lives in Middle Cottage. She moved in just over a year ago in December. She's such a lovely person and we all get on splendidly. Her boyfriend, Alec is a plumber and he's a good friend of both Marcus and me. Noelle owns Midwinter Cottage Decorations, an online business that she runs from her kitchen selling handmade decorations for all events and all seasons. She also rents a stall at the Fairlight Bay Market which is held every Thursday throughout the year. You'll find almost anything you could possibly want in that market, so I hope you find the time to visit it. I've typed out a list of places to go and things to see and do, but again, please just pop round and ring our bell if there's anything you can't find or that you want to do but it isn't on my list.'

'That's so kind, Adele,' I'd said, astonished that she had told me so much. 'I've been to Fairlight Bay before. It was ten years ago and I was only there for a week, but unless it's changed a lot over the years, I should be able to find everything I need. If I can't, I'll be sure to ask.'

I had been tempted to ask if she or her partner knew Sam Worth, but it would've been a two-edged sword. If she'd said she didn't, I'd simply have been disappointed, but if she had said she did, Sam might hear about me asking. And that was the last thing I wanted.

'I'm looking forward to meeting you, Lucy,' Adele had said. 'You're arriving on Saturday morning, is that right?'

'Yes. I only live about sixty or so miles away, in Kingston upon Thames so it shouldn't take me more than an hour and a half, depending on traffic and weather. I can call you if I'm held up or anything.'

'No. Don't worry. We'll be here all day on Saturday. Just come and ring our bell at End Cottage, or, if you'd prefer, ping me a text once you reach the car park and I'll come and meet you outside Far Cottage. It's the one on the right as you face the cottages from the car park. The one with the red post box outside.'

Now, a pair of magpies landed on that post box and I smiled as I remembered that two magpies brought joy. Or so the rhyme predicted. They screeched a loud caw-caw-caw as I neared the fence and flew off before I reached them, but I could hear them chattering as I strolled up the front path. I remembered I was supposed to send a text when I arrived, so I dropped my bags on the ground at the front door, and did that.

Having sent the text, I peered through one of the windows, but only a second or two later, I saw from the corner of my eye, a woman in her forties, together with a man about the same age come out of End Cottage. I assumed they must be Adele and Marcus and I was obviously correct.

'Hello, Lucy,' she called out and waved. 'I'm Adele and this is Marcus. Did you have a good journey?'

'Yes thank you,' I called back, as the door of Middle Cottage opened and a very pretty woman in her thirties, a handsome man not much older, and a young girl, stepped outside.

'Oh, hello.' The woman greeted me with a friendly smile. 'You must be Lucy. We're Noelle, Alec, and Melody.' She pointed at all three of them in turn.

'I'm Melody, not Noelle,' the little girl clarified, grinning at me and placing her hands in Alec's and Noelle's.

'Hello,' I said, slightly overwhelmed to be meeting so many people at once. 'Yes. I'm Lucy.'

Adele and Marcus hurried up the path towards me, exchanging greetings and smiles with their neighbours, as they did so. There was a key in Adele's hand, dangling from a red ribbon, which she held out to me.

'It's lovely to meet you, Lucy. Here's the key. Is your boyfriend still at the car?' She glanced towards the car park.

'Erm. No,' I said, embarrassed that I was going to have to tell everyone that I no longer had a boyfriend. 'Change of plan, I'm afraid. It'll only be me.' I took the key from Adele.

'Oh,' Adele said, looking concerned as she handed it over. She shot a look at Marcus as if she wasn't sure what to say next, but he merely shrugged and smiled.

'It's okay,' I added. 'We're still friends. Just bad timing.'

She gave a small sigh of relief, and smiled at me.

'Tell us to mind our own business if you like,' said Noelle, 'but we're a friendly bunch so if you want some company just knock on our doors. But if you want your privacy, that's fine too. Welcome to Midwinter. Sorry we have to dash. We promised to take Melody out for pizza and the booking is for noon. Parking in town on a Saturday takes time. We'll see you later.'

'Thank you,' I said. 'Have a good lunch.' And then I smiled at Adele and Marcus as they waved their neighbours off. 'Thank you, Adele. The cottage looks lovely. It's great to meet you both.'

Marcus beamed as he wrapped an arm around Adele's waist. 'Great to meet you, Lucy. We hope you enjoy your stay. And we agree with Noelle. Don't be a stranger. Unless you want to be. Seriously, if there's anything we can do to help you have an enjoyable time, just let us know. If you'd like to join us for a glass of wine, later, pop round at six-ish, but if you'd rather do your own thing, that's fine too.'

'There's a welcome pack in the kitchen,' Adele added, 'but I can show you around if you prefer.'

'Thanks, but that's okay. I'm sure I can find everything I need, and I promised to call my mum and my best friend the moment I arrived.'

'We'll leave you to it then,' said Marcus, thankfully taking the hint, as he removed his arm from Adele's waist and took her hand in his.

'Don't forget where we are,' said Adele as Marcus led her back towards their cottage.

I opened the front door of Far Cottage, stepped inside, and placed my bags on the wood floor of the hall. They were all extremely kind and friendly people, but that had been a little overwhelming.

One thing was certain. I wasn't going to be lonely in Midwinter.

Eight

The three cottages were very similar on the outside, so I wondered if they were also similar inside. Judging by my welcome, I would probably have an opportunity to find out. I'd been invited for drinks with Adele and Marcus that evening, so if I went, I would see inside End Cottage. I had a feeling that, before the week was out, I'd also have the chance to see inside Middle Cottage.

I had seen the photos of Far Cottage online, but sometimes photos could be misleading and make things look better – or worse – than they were in reality. But when I opened the door to the sitting room, having taken off my jacket, scarf, and gloves and left them on the rack in the hall, it looked exactly as it had in those photos.

There was a wood burner that was clearly brand-new set on a gleaming tiled fireplace from the 1930s, above which was a large screen TV. A plush, rectangular rug lay in front of the hearth, and a pale oak coffee table on which a few magazines were displayed, sat on the rug. A sumptuous looking two-seater sofa with two matching chairs, all with small side tables next to them, took up most of the room, and the only other piece of furniture was a tall, pale oak bookcase filled with books. There were table lamps on each side table, and I could recall how cosy this room had looked in the photos with that wood burner lit and the table lamps switched on. Right now though, sunshine was streaming through the window, and the central heating was doing an excellent job.

The dining room opposite had a table and four chairs, together with a sideboard, all of which matched the furniture in the sitting room. The artwork on the walls was of a similar ilk to that in the rest of the house, I soon discovered.

The designer kitchen with a huge Aga that was also clearly brand-new, took my breath away. I had a feeling I would be the first person to use this kitchen, although I assumed that either Adele or Marcus had tested everything functioned as it should. The sliding doors that overlooked the garden were also, no doubt, part of the refurbishment Adele had mentioned, but I was surprised they hadn't installed bi-folds when I opened them to step outside.

The garden wasn't massive but there was

a table and four garden chairs on a pristine looking patio that led onto the lawn. The fields surrounding the cottages, separated by hedgerows bursting with berries and buds, were visible from where I stood, but the fence, bushes, and trees on the left side of the garden were far too tall for me to see into the garden of Middle Cottage. That was probably a good thing. Was there anything worse than being overlooked by neighbours? Especially if, like me, you tended to fall asleep and snore, while sunbathing on a lounger, with slices of cucumber protecting your eyes. Not that I'd be doing a lot of sunbathing in February, although today was warm enough to sit outside ... with a coat or jacket on.

I went back inside and closed the sliding doors, remembering to lock them right away.

A welcome pack sat on one of the granite counters containing a bottle of red wine, a loaf of bread, and some snacks, along with the notes Adele had mentioned. There was milk in the fridge and butter in the small butter dish. I'd stopped on the way to buy groceries, and wine, of course, so the first thing I did before going upstairs, was to unload those and put them away.

I then grabbed the rest of my bags and went to inspect the two bedrooms and the bathroom.

The bedrooms were furnished with the

same pale oak, and the bedding and accessories were light and bright, modern florals. Each room had a small dressing table and a chair, a wardrobe, and a chest of drawers.

From the window in the back bedroom, I could see into the garden next door, where an abundance of wild birds, including four magpies, were taking advantage of the plentiful food supply provided on the bird table, and in several hanging feeders. I stood and watched them for a while wondering if the two magpies I'd seen earlier were in that group of four. Two magpies meant joy, four stood for a boy. My heart did a little flip as an image of Sam popped into my head.

'Now you're being ridiculous,' I chastised myself loudly, before turning from the window and heading towards the bathroom.

The bathroom contained a top of the range white suite, and the walk-in shower had an overhead rainfall cascade in addition to a power shower. Again, I would be the first to use it, it seemed. There were built in shelves containing towels and some water related ornaments, like a little boat, a lighthouse, and a row of ceramic and brightly painted ducks. I'd never seen a duck with yellow and blue spots, but these were rather cute. It all looked exactly as it had in the photos.

Suitably impressed, I video-called Erin to tell her all about it, and to give her a little walk-around. She laughed when I told her about meeting all my neighbours and the invitation to drinks.

'The place sounds fantastic,' Erin said. 'And you were worried you might be alone this week. Are you taking them up on the invitation?'

'It is fantastic,' I replied. 'As for the drinks, I haven't made up my mind. It's kind of them to invite me, and they do seem like genuinely friendly people, but I'm not that good at making conversation with people I don't know. How long would I need to stay without appearing rude?'

'Thirty minutes at least. Maybe an hour. If they left the invitation open, why not see how you feel later? You could always send a text saying the journey and your first day have left you feeling tired but that you'd love to meet up with them later in the week.'

'You're a genius,' I told her.

'Tell that to the top brass here,' she said. 'I love my job but I hate all the bureaucracy and the politics involved in policing.

'Bad day?'

'Nah. Just me missing you. And I'm working this afternoon and all evening until midnight, and again tomorrow, so that stinks. Bumped into Sam yet?' Erin added, laughing.

'Haha. Very funny. I wish you were here.'

'I wish that too. But someone must solve crime, and that someone is me.' She winked. 'And we're not all lucky enough to be able to take time off at a moment's notice. Call me later. Or tomorrow, if you decide to go for drinks.'

After chatting with Erin, I phoned my mum and stepdad, before realising my stomach was rumbling. I could've cooked myself some lunch but decided I would venture into Fairlight Bay and have lunch there instead.

I recalled Noelle saying that parking in town on a Saturday took time, and she would know all the best places to park whereas I would have to search for them. It was such a beautiful day, so I decided to walk. I'd checked the map and it didn't look that far.

I threw my jacket, scarf, and gloves back on and headed towards the wooden bridge.

From the car park, the lane I'd driven up earlier, led back down to a fork, and one of those was the way to Fairlight Bay. But there was also a footpath that took a route across the fields and hills and that would be much shorter, so I followed that rather than take the lane.

Despite all the recent rain, the ground

was firm underfoot and the walk was pleasant and peaceful, only improved by the wonderful birdsong that serenaded me most of the way. Although the path was longer than I'd anticipated and I was pleased to finally reach the town. I was also glad I'd worn my low-heeled ankle boots today.

Memories came flooding back and I recognised several buildings, shops, and restaurants as I walked. I spotted Fairlight Bakes Café, where Adele had told me she worked as a waitress, and I noticed it had a bakery attached. That was clearly where the Artisan loaf in my welcome pack had been baked. I now knew where to come each day if I wanted freshly baked bread. Or perhaps I could simply ask Adele to bring some back with her after her shifts. Or would that be rather cheeky? I didn't recall seeing the place the last time I was in Fairlight Bay, but at eighteen, bread had been the last thing on my mind. Especially after I'd met Sam. Its navy and white frontage looked pristine, but the swinging signage of a baker and some bread could easily have been ten years old, or more. I could simply ask Adele the next time I saw her.

The town was heaving with people, the glorious weather having no doubt brought everyone out after so many dreary days of nothing but rain. Assuming Fairlight Bay had experienced similar weather to that in Kingston upon Thames. So much for getting away from the hustle and bustle of my own town. I don't remember this place being that busy the last time I was here.

I stopped and admired the window display of a bridal shop called Fairlight Brides. That was definitely a new addition. It was smaller than the shop I helped run with my mum, but the window display was equally impressive. I couldn't stop the loud and lengthy sigh from escaping. Would I ever be a bride?

'You'd looked beautiful in that dress.' I was lost in my thoughts and I hadn't seen the elderly woman, and her little Dachshund, approach until she stood beside me and spoke. 'When's the big day?'

'What? Oh! Erm. There isn't one. That is, I'm not engaged.'

'Forgive me, my dear.' Her expression was apologetic, tinged with a hint of sadness. 'My hubby always says I shouldn't jump to conclusions. But there was a look on your face that ... Oh well. There's no harm in dreaming, is there?'

I snorted somewhat derisively. 'I don't even have a boyfriend now, so there probably is.' I hadn't intended to be rude, so I forced a smile. 'We broke up a couple of days ago, but we're still friends. The reason I was admiring the dress was because it's similar to one I designed. My mum and I own a bridal shop in Kingston upon Thames, and an online business together, and I design a few wedding dresses from time to time.'

'Well I never,' the woman said, her eyes wide and her smile matching. 'I run a bridal shop too. This one, as it happens.' She chuckled and, although I might have imagined it, so did her dog. But perhaps he was simply chomping on the toy he was holding in his mouth. 'What a small world!'

'It's a beautiful shop.'

'Thank you, my dear. Are you here on holiday? You mentioned Kingston upon Thames. My hubby took me there once, many years ago now. We went to the Royal Park at Richmond, and took a boat trip to Hampton Court. We often said we'd go back, but we haven't done so yet.'

'That's a shame,' I said. 'And yes. I'm here on holiday. I'm renting a cottage in Midwinter.'

She glanced up towards Midwinter Ridge. 'On Midwinter Lane?' Her grey brows knit together and her silver curls danced as she shook her head. 'Stock up on provisions, my dear. There's a blizzard on the way.'

'Really?' I looked up at the bright blue sky and then closed my eyes at the sun, feeling the warmth of it on my face. A blizzard seemed highly unlikely. Even rain didn't seem possible today.

'Mark my words.' Her tone was serious, and when I opened my eyes and met hers, I could see she was sincere. Even her Dachshund shook his head, his long ears flapping as if he were shaking off the bitter cold to come. 'We'll have snow this weekend.'

'Thanks for the warning. I'll be sure to stock up.' My stomach rumbled as if on cue, and I laughed. 'I arrived today and I was on my way to have lunch. It was lovely to meet you.'

'It was lovely to meet you too,' she said. 'I'm Tilly, and this is Billy.' She grinned. 'My hubby's name is Willy.'

I almost spat out a laugh. 'I'm Lucy,' I replied, maintaining as much of my composure as I could.

'Pop in for a cup of tea if you're passing this way again.'

'Thank you. That would be lovely. Weather permitting, of course.'

She winked at me and smiled as she took out a bunch of keys and slid one into the lock of her shop door, having clearly closed for lunch, and probably, to walk her Dachshund, Billy.

'You'll see,' she said, stepping inside with Billy trotting in behind her. 'Just make sure you're snowed in with someone you like.'

'Chance would be a fine thing,' I replied, waving as I turned to walk away.

Market Square was just ahead, although there wasn't an actual market as such, there today. And it wasn't really a square. The market was only held on Thursdays, although I remember Sam saying that during the festive season it was held on Saturdays too, and Market Square was more of a rectangular shape, with shops dotted around the edges.

Still smiling from my encounter with Tilly and Billy, and wondering what Willy looked like, I made my way towards the promenade. When I was last in Fairlight Bay the promenade housed several shops and restaurants. It would be lovely to have lunch overlooking the sea on a beautiful day like today. Although inside a restaurant rather than outside. The sun was shining, but a slight chill hung in the air as I walked towards the sea. Or perhaps I was imagining that.

Fairlight Bay Sailing Club, the place where I had first met Sam, sat in the middle of the long expanse of the paved promenade. It was a three-storey building with a shop front on the promenade level, an upper storey with the clubhouse and a wide balcony on which members could sit, and a lower storey where the boats and sails and all the ancillary equipment was stored. Large metal doors opened from here, onto a long concrete boat ramp that sat atop the pebbled beach and led right down into the sea.

Sam had not only been a member of the sailing club, but a sailing instructor when I met him, so I didn't want to go as far as the sailing club today, just in case, by some quirk of fate, I should bump into him. Seeing him again after all these years, on my first day here, would be difficult to say the least.

I kept as far away as I could, and selected the first restaurant I came across, which happened to be Freddie's Fish and Chips. It had certainly changed since I was last here. It was just a fish and chip shop, as the name suggested, ten years ago. Now, it was far grander, and twice the size, having taken over the shop next door, which I believed had been a souvenir shop. In addition to fish and chips, the rather impressive menu offered lobster, crab, and oysters. It also had a wine list. I was glad I'd chosen not to drive.

'Have you booked?' the smiling waitress asked me the moment I stepped inside the door. Like the town, the place was heaving. The waitress, and all the staff, were dressed in white and navy outfits, a bit like a sailor suit. Some of the females wore skirts and some wore trousers with their tops, and although they all looked smart, the uniform was also a little twee, I felt.

'Erm. No. Sorry. I only arrived in town today.'

She scanned the spacious but packed restaurant.

'As you can see, we're busy,' she said, her smile fixed in place. 'But if you don't mind waiting at the bar, I'll have a table free in about fifteen minutes. Are you on your own or will anyone be joining you?'

'I'm on my own,' I said, feeling like a wallflower at a dance. Even though my stomach had been rumbling since I'd left Far Cottage, I suspected everywhere would be the same, and fifteen minutes wasn't that long. 'And I'm happy to wait.'

'Then follow me.' She led me to the bar which ran along one side of the restaurant. 'Sit anywhere you like,' she said, handing me a little wooden boat with a number painted on the wooden sail, that she had taken from a large wooden chest at this end of the bar.

'Thanks,' I said, searching for a free bar stool and finally spotting one at the far end of the bar. Although having seen that the number on my sail was twenty-four, I felt a fifteen-minute wait might've been optimistic.

The empty seat was the other side of a stunningly beautiful woman, who sat sideways to the bar and was therefore facing in my direction. As I made my way through the crowd, I couldn't help but notice her – and I wasn't the only one. Several people, both male and female appeared to be glancing in her direction. She certainly stood out from the crowd. She wore a red dress with a tightly fitted cross over bodice, showing off her ample cleavage, and the slit to one side of the skirt, exposed her long and shapely legs. She wore high heeled, black leather ankle boots, and an open-fronted, black leather jacket. Instantly, I thought of a model in one of those TV ads for sexy and expensive perfumes. I also felt totally inadequate. She kept flicking her long blonde, wavy hair and then throwing her head back and laughing, her full red lips pouting perfectly in between. Her companion was clearly very amusing.

He was facing her, so I could only see his back, and he needed a haircut. His somewhat messy looking hair, which under the lights above the bar, looked like dark chocolate, brushed the neck of his black leather biker jacket.

The rest of him, however, from the little I could see, was as impressive as the woman. His broad shoulders, firm shapely bum, and, as I got closer, faded jeans encasing long toned legs, made me take a quick gulp of breath.

A sudden rush of heat swept through me and then, to my surprise, the man stood up and stepped right into my path. I tried to stop but my body still appeared to be moving forward and I thudded into his back with a resounding 'thrump'.

His tall frame was as solid as a wall, and he didn't even tip forward by a fraction as my body hit his, but he quickly turned and faced me, towering above me by at least one and a half feet.

'I'm so sorry,' he said, his deep voice sounding genuinely apologetic as he scanned my face, his brown eyes filled with concern. 'Are you okay? That was my fault entirely. I should've looked before I ... stepped ... out. I...' His dark brows knit together and his voice trailed off, his shapely lips still parted, mid-sentence.

I took in his firm jaw line with a hint of stubble on his handsome, weather-tanned face, and my own mouth fell open as recognition dawned, but no words came out.

'Lucy!' he added in a tone of incredulity. 'Is it ... can it really be ... you?'

Nine

'Sam!'

I couldn't believe my eyes. Or my luck.

Of all the restaurants in Fairlight Bay, of which there were several for such a small town, we had both chosen, Freddie's Fish and Chips, today.

'It is you,' he continued, looking so pleased to see me I almost threw myself into his arms. 'My god. It's been ten years and yet you haven't changed a bit. You look ... fantastic.'

His eyes travelled the length of my body from top to toe and back again and then that devastatingly gorgeous smile I remembered so well, spread across his generous mouth sending tingles of delight – and of lust – right through me.

'You look pretty good yourself,' I said, not having intended to say that aloud, as I struggled to drag my admiring gaze away from his body. The way his dark blue T-shirt hugged his chest beneath that jacket left little to my imagination, and once again, all those memories came flooding back. His body had been firm and toned and pretty damned hot ten years ago. Today it looked twice as impressive. And oh so appealing.

I coughed to try to regain my self-control.

'Thanks,' he replied, his eyes twinkling mischievously. 'What're you doing here?'

'Waiting for a table.' I couldn't think of anything brilliant to say, as usual.

He grinned at me. 'I meant, here in Fairlight Bay.' And then the grin broadened, and a hint of something danced in his eyes. 'Are you here on holiday?'

For a second or two, silence filled the narrow space between us, as my eyes bore into him, and his eyes seemed to bore right into my soul.

Were we both remembering my last holiday here, ten years ago?

I know I was.

'Yes,' I eventually managed. 'I'm here on holiday. Well, in Midwinter, strictly speaking.'

He smiled again and then furrowed his brows. 'Why Midwinter?'

Still trying to regain some composure, I shrugged as nonchalantly as I could. 'Why not?'

'No reason, I suppose.' He slowly shook

his head and a thick lock of hair brushed his cheek on one side of his face.

His hairstyle was called a messy cowlick. I remembered that from the time Erin and I had scanned the pages of a style magazine for men at our hairdresser's one day a couple of weeks earlier. We'd both laughed at that and then had a lengthy discussion as to why such a sexy hairstyle would be given such an unsexy name.

Like the model in that magazine, Sam's dark hair was shoulder length with a vague, there-but-not-there side parting, and a sort of long fringe swept back from his face.

Sandra, our hairdresser, informed us that men with this style would use wax to keep their locks in place, giving a type of wild and windswept look without the curtain of hair falling in front of their eyes.

But Sam's looked natural and product free and it took every ounce of restraint I had not to reach up and run my hands through his hair.

The beautiful woman, whom I'd completely forgotten about, coughed, and stood up, linking her arm through Sam's, somewhat possessively.

'Aren't you going to introduce me to your ... *friend*?'

The slight hesitation and then the inflection on the word friend made it sound as though she saw me as an enemy.

'What?' Sam dragged his gaze from me having also momentarily, it seemed, forgotten his stunning companion. 'Oh, yes. Sorry. Erm. Jenna, this is Lucy. Lucy, meet Jenna.'

I might have been imagining it, but I thought I detected a hint of irritation in his voice.

'Hello, Jenna,' I said, throwing her as friendly a smile as I could muster.

'Hello back, Lucy.' Her smile was definitely forced. 'And how do you know Sam?'

He looked at me and I looked at him.

'We were ... friends, once,' I said, the question having been directed at me. 'Many years ago.'

I saw his brows come together. 'Lucy was here on holiday. Ten years ago. I ... taught her how to sail.'

That sounded rather matter of fact, despite his hesitation, and I was tempted to add that he taught me a *lot* more than that. But I was pretty certain Jenna wouldn't want to hear about it.

'How long will you be in Midwinter?' Jenna asked.

'A week,' I replied, taking a quick glance at Sam to see if he reacted.

'Just a week?' he queried.

I nodded. Was I imagining the disappointment in his eyes?

'When did you arrive?' Jenna shot a look at Sam as she spoke.

As did I when I answered. 'Today. About an hour or so ago.'

'Well,' said Jenna, moving forward. 'This was nice. But we should go Sam, or we'll be late.'

'What? Oh, yeah. Erm.' Sam's frown turned into a smile. 'We must have a drink and catch up, Lucy. Give me your number and I'll call you. It's been a long time.'

'Yes, it has,' I said, catching the flash of anger in Jenna's eyes.

'Sam!' Both Sam and I looked at Jenna, who quickly smiled. 'Lucy might have a boyfriend, or something. And you can't just demand you have a drink together after not seeing one another for ten years.' She laughed, but it was obvious she wasn't amused.

'I don't,' I hurriedly said. 'Have a boyfriend.' That made me sound sad and pathetic, so I hastily added. 'I did have one. But we broke up last week.'

Sam looked relieved, but again, I might've been imagining that. Wishful thinking is a powerful thing.

'Sorry,' he said, sounding anything but, as he smiled at me.

'No need,' I replied. 'It was amicable. We're still friends.' Why did I keep saying that? Ted and I were unlikely to hang out together now that we had split up.

'Sam,' said Jenna, tugging his arm with hers. 'We'll be late. Come on.'

'Table twenty-four,' the waitress called out. 'Your table's ready.'

'I've got to go,' said Sam, his gaze fixed on my face.

'My table's ready,' I replied, standing in his way.

'It was so good to see you again, Lucy.'

'It was good to see you too, Sam.'

He lingered for a moment and then he smiled and stepped to the side of me.

'And I'd love that drink,' I quickly added. 'If you still want to catch up.'

'I do,' he said eagerly, beaming at me, as Jenna glowered at us both.

I suppose I shouldn't have sounded quite so keen. But what was the point in pretending? I'd told myself over the years that if I ever did see Sam again, I'd act cool and uninterested. I'd be aloof and mysterious, or some such rubbish like that. Instead, I'd jumped at the first opportunity to spend some time with him. I didn't know if he was single, dating Jenna, or even married. Maybe I should've asked. And perhaps I should've felt guilty, but I didn't. I reeled off my number and he tapped it into his phone. I just hoped, if we did meet for a drink, he didn't bring Jenna with him.

'I'll call you later,' he said.

'I can't wait,' I replied.

'Sam!' Jenna snapped.

He sighed. 'I've got to go, Lucy. Enjoy your lunch. I'll see you soon.'

'I hope so, Sam.'

And once again, as I had done ten years ago, I watched him walk away from me – but this time he had a stunningly beautiful woman hanging onto his arm. A woman I could never compete with.

And yet, this time there was more than a smidgen of hope in my heart, especially when he turned to look back at me and he smiled that devastating smile, before Jenna literally dragged him out of the door.

Ten

The last thing I wanted to do now was eat.

What I really wanted to do was call Erin and tell her all about bumping into Sam. But I remembered she was on shift this afternoon and all evening, and unfortunately for me, solving serious crimes took precedence over my love life.

Instead, I followed the waitress as we weaved our way through the restaurant to a table by the window. I removed my jacket and hung it over the back of my chair, having slipped my scarf and gloves into one of the large, side pockets. Once seated I read the menu, my mind still half on Sam and Jenna and only partly on what I wanted for lunch.

Eventually, I ordered skate in a samphire sauce with winter vegetables and chips, together with a large glass of white wine. Then I stared out of the window, at nothing in particular, as people walked along the promenade in both directions, and the greeny-blue sea beyond gently lapped at the sandy shore of Fairlight Bay.

My skin tingled and my heart beat faster as I remembered the days and nights I'd spent with Sam on that beach, and in several other places, and how wonderful it had felt to have Sam's arms around me. Was there even the slightest possibility that I might feel those strong yet tender arms around me again, anytime soon?

Jenna was far, far prettier than me. There was no point in denying that. And so much sexier than I could ever hope to be. Plus, she and Sam were clearly in some sort of relationship, otherwise she wouldn't have slipped her arm through his. And they were obviously going somewhere together – somewhere neither of them wanted to be late for, so that wasn't looking good for me.

And yet, Sam hadn't introduced her as his girlfriend, and from the way she had behaved, I was fairly certain that, if she had been his girlfriend, she wouldn't have hesitated to say so. All she had said was that I might have a boyfriend. She hadn't said, 'Sam, I'm your girlfriend and you shouldn't be asking other women out for a drink.' Or anything along those lines.

Although, Sam hadn't asked me out, exactly, he'd merely suggested we should go for a drink to catch up. Perhaps that didn't bother Jenna, and she would hardly see me as competition.

Of course, he might not even call. Men often said they'd call and then didn't, in my experience. And in Erin's. It was something that bugged us both.

'Why do men say they're going to call if they've got no intention of doing so?' I'd asked Erin on more than one occasion.

'It's so bloody annoying,' Erin frequently said. 'If I had my way, it would be a crime. The crime of lying and leading women on. It's not as though they have to say they'll call, is it? I mean, it's not written in stone that all men must say those words to every woman they meet.'

And almost as bad as that was the fact that Sam hadn't said when he would call. Just that he'd call me later. What did that mean? Later today? Sometime tomorrow? Later in the week?

I was going around in circles, so when the waitress brought the wine, I drank it down within seconds, and asked for a second glass.

I glanced around the restaurant, trying to think of something other than Sam, but all that did was made me realise I seemed to be the only person in there who would be eating alone.

There were tables occupied by couples, tables occupied by friends, tables occupied by families, but only one person occupied my table – me – on my own.

Thankfully, no one else, other than my waitress who smiled at me when she brought the wine, appeared to be that interested in me. The story of my life.

Even so, I turned my chair slightly so that I was directly facing the window and not the empty seat opposite me, and sipped my second glass of wine as I tuned out the cacophony of voices around me, and stared at the throng of people outside, and then across the expanse of the English Channel, and the boats, and ships, traversing the busiest shipping lane in the world.

'Would you mind some company?' a voice behind me asked a few minutes later.

I quickly swivelled in my chair and turned to face a smiling waiter.

'I'm sorry. What?'

'I asked if you would mind some company,' he repeated, his smile, like the waitress's, firmly fixed in place. 'As you can see, we're rather busy today. But please say if you'd prefer to eat alone. It's just that this is the only table with a seat free, and as it happens, there's another single person here today.'

He said it as though single people were a rarity. Perhaps they were in this restaurant. Or even in this town.

'You're asking me if someone can join me?' I queried.

He nodded, still smiling.

'Male or female?'

The smile faltered a fraction. 'Male. Is that a problem?'

'Erm. No.' I looked around but I couldn't see anyone nearby so I assumed that the person had probably been sent to wait at the bar, as I had. I was about to say it was okay, despite not really feeling okay about it at all but deciding it would be churlish to say no, and then my phone rang before I could continue. The screen display said, 'unknown number', so I raised a finger in the air to ask the waiter to give me a minute. 'Hello,' I said.

'Hello, Lucy.'

'Sam?' I couldn't believe it was him and yet I recognised his voice from earlier.

'I said I'd give you a call. I decided now was as good a time as any.' He gave a small cough. 'May I join you for lunch? I'm hoping you'll say yes, but it's fine if you say no. Well, not fine, exactly, but I'll understand if you'd rather be on your own.'

'Sam?' I repeated. 'But you left. With Jenna. You had somewhere to be.'

'I did. Now I don't. May I join you?'

'Yes!' I shrieked, waving at the waiter and nodding like a buffoon. 'Absolutely.'

'Excellent. Then I'll see you in five

minutes.'

'Five minutes? But ... aren't you waiting at the bar?'

'No.' He laughed. 'I'm at a friend's house. I'm about to get on my bike.'

'Your bike? You ... you're cycling here?'

'Cycling?' He laughed louder. 'Nope. Motorbike.'

I laughed too, but I felt rather foolish. Of course it would be a motorbike and not a bicycle. What was I thinking?

'Are you bringing Jenna?' He'd said he was at a friend's house; I assumed it was hers.

'Jenna? No.' He sounded as confused as I was. 'I'll see you soon.'

He rang off just as the waiter approached with a man following him, and I realised I'd made a huge mistake. When I'd answered my phone, I'd incorrectly thought it was Sam who'd asked if he could join me, not a total stranger. I shook my head at the waiter and the smile faded from his lips.

'I'm so sorry,' I said as he neared my table. 'I thought it was ... a friend. Erm. This seat's not vacant, after all. My friend is coming to join me.'

The waiter glared at me but the man behind him smiled and shrugged. He was actually rather good-looking.

'Don't worry,' the stranger said in a

pleasant manner. 'These things happen. Enjoy your lunch with your friend.' He turned to the waiter. 'I can wait.'

The waiter threw me an irritated look and then that smile was back in place.

'I apologise for the confusion, sir,' he said to the man, completely ignoring me. 'I'll get you seated as soon as I can. Thank you for being so understanding.'

'Sorry,' I said again, as the pair of them went back towards the bar.

I caught the attention of my waitress and ordered another glass of wine. My third. But I needed it. I gulped down the last drops of my second glass and handed it to her when she brought the next one.

'A friend is now joining me for lunch,' I said. 'Is there any chance you could ask the chef to hold my meal until he orders? He'll be here in five minutes.'

She raised one brow, but the smile hardly faltered. 'I'm sure that won't be a problem.' The look in her eyes, however, told me otherwise.

I wasn't making any friends among the staff at Freddie's Fish and Chips.

Eleven

Having kept my eyes trained on the front door of the restaurant, and having moved my chair again in order to do so, my heart gave a little leap each time someone came in. I checked my watch every minute or so but I think I can safely say those five minutes were the longest of my life. At least that's how it felt. When Sam did eventually arrive and I watched him walk towards me, I wanted to run to him and throw myself into his arms.

Except that wouldn't have been cool, and, to be honest, after three large glasses of white wine, I wasn't sure I could walk properly, let alone run. I hadn't eaten since around eight a.m. that morning, and I'd been so excited, and also slightly anxious about spending the week on my own, that I'd only had a banana ... and several cups of coffee. The wine had gone straight to my head, and the remnants of the caffeine probably hadn't helped.

I was having palpitations and it was as if

Sam was walking in slow motion, his hair dancing around his shoulders with each step and his faded jeans and dark blue T-shirt hugging every muscle as he moved. The smile on his lips made my entire body go limp, and his eyes lit up as he finally reached my table, sending a surge of excitement from my head to my toes. I think I actually gasped.

'Hi, again,' he said, his voice soft and yet husky. He ran a hand through his hair and then he looked me in the eye as he gripped the back of the vacant chair. 'I'd planned to play it cool.' He laughed sardonically. 'That lasted all of five minutes. Seeing you again was such a surprise. I felt ... I feel ... I didn't want to wait till later. Does this sound crazy?' He let go of the chair and took a step away, and then a step towards me and then he held up his arms as if he wasn't sure what to do or say next. 'It does, doesn't it?' He laughed again and shook his head. 'I've imagined this so many times and yet, now you're here, I'm behaving like a jerk. May I sit?'

'Please do,' was all I could say.

He sat opposite me and took a deep breath and then he stared at me for a second or two.

'I still can't believe it's you. That you're here. Especially after all these years.'

'Neither can I.'

'What made you come back? And why

now?'

'Erm.' I wasn't expecting so many questions, and after all the wine I'd drunk, together with the effect just looking at him was having on me, I couldn't think clearly. 'I booked a last-minute romantic break for me and Ted. My boyfriend. My ex-boyfriend, I mean.' I shook my head in the hope that it would clear my thoughts. 'Erm. I saw the cottage in Midwinter online, and I thought it looked nice.'

He furrowed his brows as he scanned my face. 'Nothing to do with me then? With us?'

'Erm.' I must stop saying, 'erm'. It really wasn't helping. I met his intense gaze. 'Us? I … I don't think so. And yet...' I shrugged. 'Perhaps it was. I … I still think about that week … sometimes.'

'Me too.'

'Are you ready to order?' the waitress asked Sam, startling us both, having appeared from nowhere. Or so it seemed.

'What? Yes.' He looked at me.

'I've already ordered.'

'Oh. I'll have whatever my friend's having. Thanks. And a bottle of white wine, please.'

'Would that be a bottle of Sancerre, sir? That's what your friend has been drinking.' The waitress glanced at me, and at my, once again, empty glass.

'Yes. That's fine, thanks,' Sam said.

She took my glass and walked away.

'When did you break up?' Sam repositioned the cutlery at his place setting, avoiding my eyes as he spoke. 'Was the relationship serious?'

'With Ted?' Sam nodded, so I continued. 'On Thursday night. And, yes and no. We'd been dating for more than a year but ... something changed after the new year. I ... I booked this break in the hope that it might bring us back together. But all it did was made us both realise we were drifting further apart. Ted asked me to cancel. I refused. So ... he ended it. But it was sort of mutual. I'm not upset. Just, maybe, a little sad that another relationship hasn't worked out. Sorry. I'm rambling.' My cheeks flushed with embarrassment. I hadn't meant to say so much.

Sam shook his head. 'Not at all. Is that what you want then? A relationship?'

I gave a small laugh. 'Doesn't everybody?'

Sam's shrug surprised me. And yet, in a way, it didn't. But his words did.

'I don't,' he said, his eyes locked firmly on mine.

'You don't? Not at all?' I laughed nervously. 'Perhaps you just haven't met the right woman yet.'

He frowned. 'It's just not me. Relationships, I mean. Don't get me wrong. I like dating. I like having fun. But a long-term commitment isn't on the cards for me.'

'Oh. I see. I remember that's how you felt ten years ago, but I thought you might've ... changed your mind since then.'

'No. Nothing's changed.'

He was looking at me so intensely and I had a feeling he wanted to say more, but he didn't.

'And Jenna?' I couldn't help myself. I had to ask. Now it was me who felt the need to rearrange my own cutlery.

'Jenna's a friend.'

'A friend you're dating?'

'No. But we did hook up for a couple of weeks last summer. Nothing serious.'

'Because you don't have relationships?'

His eyes scanned my face. 'That's right. But Jenna still does some work for me from time to time.'

'Work? What sort of work? What do you do for a living?' I tried to make it sound casual, but even to my ears it sounded as though I was giving him a grilling. 'I seem to recall you saying work was a necessary evil, or something along those lines.'

He laughed. 'That sounds like me. After that summer, I went travelling, as I'd planned. And you went to uni.' He waved a

93

hand in the air. 'That was a lifetime ago. Anyway, I bought a bike.' He grinned. 'A motorbike. And I loved it, so when I came home, I opened a bike shop and garage. Adventure, Sport, Roadsters, Modern Classics, and Vintage. Starter bikes to top of the range. I buy, sell, and repair them all. New and used.'

'Wow. That's a surprise.' I shot a look at his hands. He clearly took care of himself. The skin was smooth and his agile fingers didn't look like those of a man who repaired motorbikes.

As if reading my mind, he said, 'I have a mechanic. But I do like to get my hands dirty from time to time.'

I remembered how good those hands had felt on my body and I wished the waitress would hurry up with that wine.

'And ... how does Jenna fit into that? You said she does some work for you from time to time.'

'Jenna? Yeah. She's one of the models I use for my ads.'

'Ads? You run ads? And have models? Crikey. You're in the big leagues.'

Again he laughed. 'I wouldn't say that. But I do okay. The ads are for the local press, my website, and for the specialist magazines. They're not on mainstream TV or anything. How about you? You wanted to be a wedding dress designer, I seem to recall.' He licked his lips as though he was nervous. Perhaps, as he didn't have relationships, the word, 'wedding' had that effect on him.

'Yes. My young dream. I do design a few, but I'm not exclusively a designer. Mum and Dad split up and Mum owns a bridal shop in Kingston upon Thames. That's where we live. I help her run the shop and we also have a thriving online business too.'

'That sounds great.'

'So ... does Jenna lounge seductively on your bikes, then? In your ads? For all the guys to drool over her.'

He snorted with laughter and shook his head, pushing back a thick lock of hair with his hand. 'Nope. She's in the ads to sell bikes to women, not guys. Although I'm sure she does both. She's a bit like the women in perfume ads. She's there to sell the dream.'

He pulled out his phone, scrolled a few pages, and then showed me a collage of Jenna in black leathers, and Jenna in a dress similar to the one she was wearing today, astride a massive beast of a bike, and Jenna standing beside a gleaming and obviously expensive bike with a gorgeous hunk of a man standing behind her, but she was clearly the one in control. Jenna was already selling the dream to me.

'Oh!' I cocked my head to one side. I'd

thought of perfume ads when I first saw her, so it was strange that Sam had used that comparison too. Or maybe not. 'She's good at her job. Would I look that sexy, powerful, and in control, if I bought a bike from you?'

He raised his brows and then a devilish smile spread across his mouth. 'You don't need to buy a bike to look like that, Lucy,' he drawled.

'Shall I pour?' the waitress asked, appearing beside us with a bottle of wine and two sparklingly clean glasses. 'Your meals will be with you momentarily.'

'That's okay, thanks,' said Sam. 'We'll do it.'

The waitress placed the bottle and the glasses on the table, and Sam began to pour the wine as she smiled and walked away.

'Where were you meant to be right now?' I asked, having been wondering how he had managed to get out of whatever it was he and Jenna had planned to do when they had left.

He shot me a look but continued filling our glasses before he answered.

'On a photoshoot, as it happens. But they didn't really need me. My team know what I want. I dropped Jenna off at Elliot's – he's a photographer, and a good mate of mine, and checked everything was okay, and then I called you, having decided I'd rather be here than there.'

Before I could respond, the waitress had returned with our meals. She really had meant they would be with us momentarily.

'Please let me know if there's anything else I can get you,' she said. 'Enjoy your meals.'

'Thanks,' Sam and I said in unison.

He held up his glass and I did likewise and we clinked them together. Although I was still trying to get my head around the fact that he'd left a photoshoot to come and have lunch with me. And that he had 'a team'. And models. And a photographer.

'Cheers,' he said. 'Here's to a great week.'

'Cheers,' I replied. 'I second that.'

We both took mouthfuls of our drinks and then he looked at me as he put down his glass.

'Do you have plans?'

'Plans? Oh, for today, you mean? I've been invited for drinks with my neighbours around six-ish, but other than that, no.'

Sam narrowed his eyes a fraction and an odd sort of smile hovered on his lips. 'For this week.'

'Oh! Erm.' I coughed to clear my throat. 'Not really. No.'

I took another sip of wine, feeling even more nervous and self-conscious than I had before.

'Would you like to spend it with me?'

I was so surprised by that question that I almost spat out my wine, but I managed to choke it back, and I somehow settled my glass onto the table without spilling a drop.

'What?'

He shrugged one shoulder. 'Feel free to say no. I won't be offended. But ... we had a great time when you were last here, didn't we? I ... hoped we could do so again.'

I could feel my jaw drop as I stared at him. Was he for real?

All I managed in response was, 'Erm.' Even that sounded more like a squeak than a word.

I grabbed my glass and took several more gulps. The last time I was here, Sam and I had spent most of the week having sex. Great sex. Fantastic sex. Mind blowing sex. But after that first day together when he taught me how to sail, we did little else but have sex. At least, nothing I could really remember right now. Is that what he was suggesting?

I shivered with anticipation, quivered with excitement, and tingled with delight at the very thought of it. All my dreams were coming true. And I'd only been in Fairlight Bay for an hour or two.

Well, perhaps not *all* my dreams. Sam had already made it clear that relationships still weren't his thing. If we spent this week together it would simply be another holiday fling for him. Could it be merely that for me? Or would I want it to be something more? It had been ten years and I still wasn't over him. Could I risk having sex with him all week, without risking my heart breaking, all over again?

'Sorry,' he said, shaking his head as he reached for his own glass. 'I could've phrased that better.' He had a quick swig and then he smiled. 'What I meant was, it would be great to spend some time with you this week. If you don't have any plans. I could show you the sights. Take you sailing. Have you sailed much since ... then?'

I shook my head. 'No. Erm. That would be nice.'

His eyes held mine. 'Yes. It would. I could give you a tour on my bike. Do you like bikes?'

I shook my head again. 'I don't know. I've never been on one.'

'Never?' His look now was one of incredulity.

'Everyone I know has a car. Apart from you. Do you have a car? Or just a bike?'

'Two bikes and a car.'

'Oh. Erm. A bike ride would be nice. I think.'

'You'd be safe. I'd make sure of that. And we could do ... other things. Anything you want to, really. I'm easy. What I mean is, I'm happy to do anything you'd like to do. I just … it would be great to … get to know you again.'

'Yes,' I said. 'That would be … great.'

Our eyes locked. My heart raced. Electricity coursed through every inch of me. But we were both avoiding talking about the one thing I was sure was on both our minds.

Sex.

'Is everything okay, here?' The waitress was back again.

'Yes,' said Sam, not taking his eyes off me. 'Everything is…'

'Great.' I finished the sentence for him, but then I dragged my eyes away. 'We should eat before this gets cold.'

'Yes,' he said. 'I suppose we should.'

Twelve

We chatted about all sorts of things while we ate. I asked him about his travels; he asked me about uni and my life in Leeds. I asked for more details about his life since then, and he asked for more about mine.

'After I returned home,' Sam said, 'I spent the first few years getting the business off the ground. I'd still got some savings, having worked whenever I got the chance while I was travelling, and my granddad passed away soon after I got back, and he left me some money.'

'Oh I'm sorry. About your granddad, not the money.'

He threw me a smile. 'Thanks. He'd been unwell for years, so in a way, it was a blessing when he went. And I was able to grow the business must faster with the help of that money. I like to think he's a part of the business, and that he's looking down and cheering me on.'

'I'm sure he is.'

'Yeah. Anyway, the Covid years were tough. For everyone, of course. But I was lucky, and afterwards, I worked even harder. I'm in a really good place now and life is ... treating me well.'

'I'm so pleased for you. And I'm glad you found a job you enjoy.'

'I enjoyed teaching people to sail,' he grinned. 'Especially you. But I love everything about bikes. Did you know that, every year, there's a bikers' rally where thousands of bikers, ride down from all over the country to Fairlight Bay? It's over the May Bank Holiday weekend, and there are literally thousands and thousands of them. Bikes, and bikers for as far as the eye can see. You should come and see it. If you're free.'

'I didn't know that. I'd love to see it.'

'Great. It's a date.' He met my eyes. 'No, not a date. An invitation. Tell me about your shop and the online business,' he said, hastily changing the subject.

I'd already told him that Mum had moved back to Kingston upon Thames when she and Dad split up, and that she owned a bridal shop.

'When Mum moved back, she got a job in the bridal shop she now owns. When the former owners decided to retire, the following year, they asked Mum if she'd like to buy their lease, and she snapped it up. I was intending to try to get a job in a fashion house specialising in bridal wear, or in a bridal boutique in London, or another big city, when I finished my degree, but as soon as Mum bought that lease, I knew where I wanted to be. So I joined her in the shop, and we expanded online. As you said, the Pandemic was a tough time, but we managed to get through it. I've designed some wedding dresses. Well, quite a few, actually. And one day I might concentrate more on the design side, rather than the retail side, but for now, I'm happy with things as they are.'

'I'd love to see some of your designs.'

I raised my brows and laughed. 'Seriously? Someone who doesn't believe in relationships, wants to see wedding dress designs?' I shook my head.

'Why not? They're just dresses, aren't they? It's the designs that interest me, not what they stand for.'

'Okay.' I took out my phone and scrolled to the photos of my own designs, some of the gowns were modelled by Erin and some by me. The first photo was of Erin. 'That's not me, that's my best friend, Erin. People say we look like twins.'

He looked at the photo and then up at me. 'You do look alike, but I wouldn't say you were twins. The dress is stunning though.' He scrolled to the next photo and gave a sharp gasp, and this time, when he looked up at me there was something in his eyes I couldn't quite fathom but it sent a frisson of excitement through me. 'You ... you make a beautiful bride.' His eyes held mine for a few moments and then he studied the photo, a small crease appearing between his brows as his jaw tightened.

'Thank you,' I said. 'There're a few more photos.'

He shot me a look and then scrolled to the next one. Another photo of me but in a different dress. This one was a rather sexy, off the shoulder, tightly fitted, and short-skirted number, leaving little to the imagination, and I might've imagined it, but I was sure his hand tightened around my phone, and his body seemed to tense. He coughed swallowed hard, coughed quickly, and rapidly scrolled to the next photo, and then the next, and then slowed down slightly once he reached another photo of Erin.

Was my heart playing tricks on me, or did he seem to find the photos of me in a wedding dress – any wedding dress – difficult to look at?

Or did he just prefer looking at Erin?

'You're very talented, Lucy.'

He handed me back my phone but as our fingers brushed, he snatched his hand away. I almost dropped the phone as I hadn't got a firm hold on it, but he was already finishing his meal, his eyes now fixed on his plate, not on me.

There was an awkward silence for a while as we both cleared our plates but as soon as we put down our cutlery, the waitress reappeared. She seemed to pop up constantly, despite how busy the restaurant was. Although there did seem to be an ample supply of staff.

'Would you like our dessert menu?'

'Not for me, thanks,' I said, reaching for my wine glass and drinking down the remaining contents.

Sam shook his head. 'Just the bill, please.' Then he refilled my glass.

'I think I've had enough,' I said, laughing to make light of how much I had drunk.

'I've got my bike. One glass is enough for me.'

That's when I realised that he had been refilling my glass and not his own. In addition to the three large glasses I'd consumed before he arrived, I'd now drunk most of the bottle.

'Are you trying to get me drunk to have your wicked way with me?'

I regretted it the second the words tumbled out of my mouth.

He frowned. 'Is that what you think?'

'No! It was a joke. You don't need to get

me drunk. I mean ... No. Although, to be completely honest, I am a little tipsy. My fault. Not yours. You see, I'd had a couple of glasses before you arrived. And I hadn't eaten anything since early this morning.'

'You don't need to explain.'

'I'm not. Erm.' I shook my head. 'Sorry.'

'What for?'

I shrugged. 'Ruining everything.'

'Cash or card?'

This waitress was getting on my nerves.

'I'll pay,' I said.

'You won't,' said Sam, handing over a gold card, keying in his pin number when asked, and then giving her a fiver for a tip.

The waitress gave him the receipt and an even bigger smile. 'I hope I'll see you again soon,' she said, ignoring me completely.

Sam got to his feet. 'Ready?'

'Yes.'

I stood up so fast I almost toppled over. Sam reached out and took my arm, and then he grabbed my jacket and wrapped it around my shoulders.

'I'd offer you a lift on my bike,' he said, a hint of amusement in his voice now. 'But you might fall off. I'll get you a cab instead. And for the record, you haven't ruined anything, Lucy. I'm just being a jerk, as usual.'

Thirteen

Why did Erin have to be on shift, today of all days?

I sent her a text the moment I closed the front door of Far Cottage.

'Please call me if you get a chance. Really need some advice. Have just had lunch with Sam!!!!!! Love you. Xx'

I shrugged off my jacket, checked my scarf and gloves were still in the pocket, and hung the jacket on the rack, then I kicked off my boots and dashed to the loo. After all that wine, I needed to pee.

Having washed my hands, and studied my reflection in the mirror to see if my cheeks were as red as they felt, which thankfully, they weren't, I made my way to the kitchen, filled the kettle, and made a cup of tea.

I had just sat on the sofa to drink it when my phone pinged with a text. It was from Erin.

'Why use one exclamation mark when

six say so much more? Just lunch? Or is that a euphemism? Will call you asap. Taking a break in ten minutes. Wait by the phone!!!!!! Love you. Xx'

I laughed despite feeling like a nervous wreck, and then I counted the minutes until I could talk to my best friend.

It had only been about four until her name appeared on my screen.

'That was a quick ten minutes!'

'Time flies in The Met,' she said. 'Tell me everything.'

I told her how I'd bumped into Sam at the bar, how he'd looked, what he'd said, what Jenna had said, and everything else I could remember. I told her Sam had said he'd call and I'd driven myself half mad wondering when he might, even though he'd only just left, and then how he had called and how happy I was. I told her about the mix up with the stranger and the table, and then how Sam had made me feel when he'd arrived, about our conversation, the waitress and her constant interruptions, the wedding dress photos, Sam's business, what he'd said about not having relationships, how he'd asked if I wanted to spend the week with him, and then how he had brought me back to Far Cottage, in a cab.

'I've had a lot of wine, so I can't recall it all word for word, but I've told you as much as I can. So what do you think?'

'I think one of us will be having rampant sex this week, and unfortunately it won't be me.'

'Oh god, I hope so,' I said. 'I thought I'd blown it for a minute, but when he dropped me off, he asked the driver to wait, and he walked me to the door and waited until I'd opened it and stepped inside.'

'Didn't you ask him in?' Erin sounded surprised.

'Of course I did. But he said he had to go.'

'What else did he say? How were things left?'

'He didn't say much in the cab. He just pointed out places we'd gone together ten years ago. But when he walked me across the bridge, he linked my arm through his and said that he needed to go and check that the photoshoot had gone as planned. And then he said that he had to meet his dad this evening, for a drink, and that he couldn't get out of that because his dad had told him he needed to ask him something important. I said that was fine, and that I might have a nap this afternoon.'

Erin's snort of laughter made me stop talking. 'You told a sexy hunk of a guy that you needed a nap in the afternoon?'

'No! I didn't say I *needed* a nap. I said I might *take* a nap. There's a big difference.'

'If you say so.' She laughed.

'I do. And then I added that I'd been invited for drinks with the neighbours around six-ish, so he said he'd call me later.'

'Did he kiss you?'

'No. Well, yes. But only on the cheek. And it was more a brush of his lips against my skin than an actual kiss. But even that almost threw me into a frenzy of desire. If the cab driver hadn't been waiting in the car parking area, I might well have dragged Sam inside and demanded sex on the spot. Why does he have to be so bloody hot? Anyway, I'm back to square one, aren't I? Back to waiting for him to call me. Or not.'

'He'll call.'

'How can you be sure? Don't forget, I had too much wine. I said some stupid things. And, more importantly, he only wants sex.'

'Don't we all,' Erin said with a sigh. 'And, I may be wrong, but didn't you just say you wanted to have sex with him in the hall. Pot calling the kettle black, don't you think?'

I tutted loudly. 'Okay. I admit I'm lusting after him. What I mean is, all Sam wants is another holiday fling, whereas I want something more. It's been ten years and I'm still getting over the last one. Do I want to do this again, knowing that it might take me another ten years to get over him? Assuming

I ever could. And having been with him today, I think it'll be even harder this time. Getting over him, I mean. Might I be better off not having sex with him? Not seeing him again?'

'And miss out on all that fantastic sex? Are you mad? Besides, I think the damage is already done, isn't it? You want to spend the week with him, don't you?'

'Of course I do. But I also want a relationship. I want someone to love me, Erin. I want someone I can build a future with. I can't do any of that with Sam. He's made that perfectly clear.'

'I love you,' she said, and blew me a loud and slobbery-sounding kiss. 'But I hear what you're saying, and yes, it's a concern. Okay. Here's what I think you should do. See this week as a final hurrah. Your goodbye to Sam, the past, and all things Sam-related. Have as much fun this week as you possibly can, but keep your heart out of the equation. Keep reminding yourself that this is purely a fling. Purely sex. And tell yourself that, as soon as you come home, you're going to make a determined effort to find Mr Right. To find the guy you're going to spend the rest of your life with. And that Sam Worth will be history after this week. No matter what. You can do it, Lucy. I know you can. Go into this with your eyes wide open, and don't let him into your heart, just your bed.'

'That's easy for you to say.'

'I know. But if you don't sleep with him this week, you'll only regret it. And let's be honest, you know you're going to, anyway, so why are we even discussing it? Just make sure that you keep your feelings out of it.'

'Again, easy for you to say. But you're right. I can't spend this week here without seeing Sam. So I'll put on my big girl's pants and pull up the drawbridge to my heart, or some such crap, and I'll have sex with him on my terms, not on his.'

'Good for you. I should be off by midnight, so if you need to call me later, you can, but if I don't hear from you tonight, I'll call you tomorrow for an update. Just sex, remember. Love has no part in this. Your heart is under lock and key. And speaking of locks and keys, I suppose I'd better go and find some good for nothings to throw in jail. And you'd better go and have that nap.' Erin laughed as she rang off.

I wasn't sure why my taking a nap was so funny, but as hard as I tried to stay awake, I dozed off on the sofa. It was almost five when I awoke and my hair was a disaster.

I checked my phone, just in case, but other than a text from Mum saying she hoped I was having a lovely time, no one else had contacted me.

I decided I had two options. Have a shower, put on something sexy, or at least something that looked good, and then sit and wait for Sam to call, in the hope he'd suggest we meet up later. Or do the shower and dress thing and then go to join Adele and Marcus for that drink.

As I was doing this my way, the drink with the neighbours was the way to go.

Naturally, I checked my phone again when I got out of the shower – and tossed it on the bed. Then quickly picked it up again and checked the battery life. To be safe, I put it on charge before I did my hair and got dressed.

As this was originally supposed to be a romantic getaway for Ted and me, I had bought a few new items of clothing, including some sexy underwear. When I knew it was going to be me on my lonesome, I had planned to leave the underwear at home, but Erin had convinced me to bring it.

'You might get lucky,' she had said on Friday night, 'and you'd hate yourself if all you had to wear were plain cotton knickers and two-year-old bras. Or you might be in an accident, and again, no one wants to see old undies. Take the underwear with you. And take the new togs too. Just in case.'

So I had packed the lot. And yet again, Erin had been right.

I was so glad I always took her advice. Well, almost always.

The black lace matching set did wonders for my self-esteem, and the black stockings added to that feeling. As did the fitted black crepe wrap dress which looked better on me this evening than it had in the shop when I'd tried it on last week. I had tied my blonde hair into a loose, low chignon, and I painted my nails a deep, glossy red to match my lipstick. The only jewellery I wore was a pair of pearl drop earrings, and my watch.

I took a final look at my reflection and I breathed in a satisfied smile.

I really hoped Sam would call and arrange to meet up later. I couldn't remember the last time that I was pleased with the way I looked.

But I wasn't pleased that it was six-fifteen. Where had the time gone?

I raced downstairs, grabbed one of the bottles of white wine I'd brought with me, from the fridge, and hurried into the hall. I slipped my feet into my ankle boots, threw on my jacket, and opened the front door. An arctic blast of air took my breath away. It was absolutely freezing out there.

Tilly, the elderly woman I'd met had predicted snow, and her words came rushing back to me, along with an icy gust of wind. "Stock up on provisions, my dear. There's a blizzard on the way."

It was dark outside; I'd forgotten how dark it gets in the countryside as opposed to the towns. Thankfully the streetlamps in Midwinter Lane, and in the car parking area opposite, provided enough light for me to see my way to End Cottage, and also to see that, although it was bitterly cold, there was no sign of any snow. At least, not yet.

I hurried down the path, hugging my jacket around me, dashed along the lane, and up the path to the front door of End Cottage. I rang the bell and a second or two later, Marcus flung open the door, smiling in greeting.

'Come in, Lucy.' He gestured me inside with his hands. 'It's freezing out there. I just popped outside to put some rubbish in the bin and I got the shock of my life after the sunshine and warmth we had today.'

He closed the door behind me as Adele stepped into the hall.

'Hello,' she said, smiling. 'Can you believe this weather? But it is still February, after all.'

'It was a gorgeous day, wasn't it?' I said. 'But I met a woman called Tilly in town, and she told me we'd have snow this weekend. I thought she was joking. Now I think she might be right. It's lovely and warm in here though.'

'It's certainly cold enough for snow,' Adele agreed.

'It's highly likely,' Marcus said. 'Let me take your jacket.'

I handed Marcus the bottle of wine, and he smiled without even glancing at the label. I hate it when people look at the label, as if they're checking whether you've brought plonk, and not a decent bottle, so that made me like him more than I already did.

'Thank you,' he said. 'That's good of you.'

I took off my jacket and he hung it up on a rather posh rack.

'This way,' he said. 'We've got a couple of bottles of white, and also red, open, so which would you prefer?'

'White, please. Although, I had a few glasses at lunch, so I'd better just have one.'

'One at a time, you mean?' he laughed as did Adele, and I joined in because their laughter was infectious.

A bell chimed, and Marcus turned back towards the door. 'That'll be Noelle, Alec, and Melody. We asked them to join us. Follow Adele into the sitting room and make yourself at home.'

'I hope Far Cottage is warm enough,' Adele said. 'If not, just shout.'

'It's perfect, thanks,' I assured her as I stepped into a spacious, open plan sitting and dining room.

Anyone would admire the sleek lines, expensive furniture and furnishings, and original artwork on the walls, and over to one side was a designer kitchen Erin and I would both kill for. The place was remarkably similar to Far Cottage, even down to the glass, sliding doors the width of the back wall. So Marcus had clearly redesigned Adele's former home to a virtual replica of the home they now shared.

There was a TV on one wall that was three times the size of the one I had at home – and I thought mine was large – and the surround sound speakers were as stylish as the rest of the furniture. I wondered if the upstairs was also almost identical to Far Cottage. But I didn't want to ask.

Noelle, Alec, and Melody were laughing as they came in with Marcus.

'Hello again, Lucy,' Noelle said. 'I hear you met Tilly today. She's a character, isn't she? So we're in for a blizzard, I hear.'

I thought she was making fun of me – or of Tilly, but I soon realised she wasn't.

'You told me she's always right,' Alec said to Noelle, as he swept Melody up in his arms. 'So it looks like we might be making snowmen tomorrow, sweetheart.' He planted a big kiss on the little girl's cheek and she giggled loudly and melodically.

'Snow people, Daddy,' Melody corrected.

Alec winked at me as he placed her back on the ground. 'My apologies. Snow people. If you're not busy tomorrow, Lucy, feel free to join us.'

'Do you really think we'll have snow?' I queried as Marcus handed me a glass of wine. A large glass of wine.

'Yes.' They all spoke in unison, as Marcus poured wine for everyone else, and then for himself.

'If Tilly says it'll snow,' said Adele. 'It'll snow.'

Noelle nodded. 'She and her husband, Willy, are the ones to ask if you want to know about the weather. But I hope it's not a blizzard. Getting snowed in for your week away isn't ideal, is it, Lucy?'

I grinned. 'Tilly said I should make sure I am snowed in with someone I like.'

Everyone laughed at that, but they all nodded, even Melody. Although I don't think she understood the real meaning behind that comment.

Marcus raised his glass. 'Here's to new friends, and to neighbours, and to being snowed in with people we like.'

We all raised our glasses and said, 'Cheers', to that.

'And to snow people,' Melody added, her glass of fruit juice still raised.

'And to snow people,' we all agreed,

raising our glasses once again.

I wished Sam was with us. But I hadn't heard a word from him.

It would be just my luck that I'd get snowed in up here on Midwinter Ridge, and Sam would be snowed in down in Fairlight Bay.

So near, and yet so far.

Again, the story of my life.

It wasn't until more than an hour later, during our conversations, when I'd told them all I designed wedding dresses, and that I helped my mum run a bridal shop and an online business, and Noelle asked to see some photos of the dresses I'd designed, that I remembered I'd left my phone on charge in my bedroom in Far Cottage.

Emily Harvale

Fourteen

I'd told myself I would only have one glass of wine. I'd also told Marcus the same thing. And yet I lost count after the third, I think. But once I'd realised I hadn't got my phone, and the ramifications of that fact had fully dawned on me, I seemed to sober up.

More so when Melody screamed out joyfully that it was snowing, and pointed to the large flakes falling into the back garden of End Cottage, lit up by the outside lights on Marcus and Adele's patio.

'I've had a lovely time,' I said, getting slowly to my feet, unsure of how steady I might be. 'But I'm expecting a call from ... a friend, and my phone's on charge in the cottage, so I think I'd better say a huge thank you for this evening, and make my way back. We were ... supposed to be meeting up later. I think.'

'Oh that's a shame,' said Adele, sounding genuinely sad I was leaving. 'But do pop round again whenever you like. And feel free to bring your friend.'

'Is this someone you'd like to be snowed in with?' Noelle asked, as if reading my mind.

Heat rushed to my cheeks. 'Well, I wouldn't say no,' I said, regretting it immediately.

'Oooh,' said Adele, jumping up from her armchair. 'Is it someone in Fairlight Bay?'

Now my cheeks were burning.

'It's someone I knew a long time ago,' I said, moving towards the door.

'Between us, we know almost everyone in town,' Adele informed me, following close behind.

'Adele,' said Marcus, laughing, as he got to his feet. 'You're embarrassing Lucy. Leave her alone, or she won't want to come back.'

They all got up now and followed me into the hall, apart from Alec who was looking out of the front window.

'Does your friend own a motorbike?' Alec asked, popping his head around the door frame.

'Erm. Why?' I asked, unsure how to answer.

'Because one is just pulling into the parking area, and ... Oh. I recognise that bike. I think it might be Sam.'

'Sam!' I shrieked, half in delight, half in surprise.

'Sam?' Marcus queried. 'You mean Sam

Worth?'

'Of course,' said Alec, as if there wasn't anyone else called Sam in Fairlight Bay.

'Sam's your ... friend?' Noelle's eyes lit up, as did Adele's, and they exchanged knowing glances.

'Oh yes,' Adele sighed. 'I can see why you'd want to be snowed in with him.'

Marcus raised a brow, and then laughed when she blew him a kiss.

'But I'd rather be snowed you with you, my darling,' she hastily added.

'I had my photo taken on one of Sam's special bikes last summer,' said Melody, in such a matter-of-fact tone that it took the wind out of my sails and I stood and stared at her.

'You did?' I asked, unable to conceal the disbelief in my voice.

'She did,' Alec confirmed. 'It was for an ad campaign Sam was running, and the bike she was sitting on was a Ducati Panigale V4, one of the most high-performance sports bikes that's street legal. Melody was seven at the time. The next shot was of a girl called Bryony, who was thirteen, and the next was of Sara, who was eighteen, then there was Jenna. She's a model Sam often uses, and she's in her late twenties, and then came Penny. She was around thirty, and, well, you get the idea. Funnily enough, Tilly was in the final photo. She's in her seventies. The ad said something along the lines of, 'You're never too young to dream, and never too old to live that dream.'

'I'm getting a bike just like it when I grow up,' said Melody.

'We'll see,' said Alec, shaking his head at me, and mouthing the word, 'No.' But he was smiling.

'Well,' said Marcus, opening the front door, as Sam was striding across the wooden bridge, having removed his crash helmet. 'I don't think Sam's here to see any of us, is he? Although, it would be rude not to invite him in.' He met my eyes and smiled. 'But perhaps you should retrieve your phone first, and ask him if he'd like to pop in for a quick drink. We won't be offended if the two of you have other plans.'

He winked at me as he handed me my jacket, and he waved at Sam, as did everyone else behind me. Sam stopped in his tracks for a split second, before waving back.

'I'll leave the door on the catch,' said Marcus, and he closed it behind me as I stepped out onto the path and hurried towards the front fence.

From the glow of the streetlights as Sam reached the one nearest to me, I could see he was frowning, as if he wasn't sure what was going on.

'Hi,' I said. 'This is a lovely surprise.'

He looked cross. 'I've been calling you for over an hour. I thought something might've happened to you. Or that you were mad with me, or something. I see I was wrong on both counts. Is everything okay with Marcus?'

'Sorry. I left my phone on charge in the cottage and I've only just realised. I was on my way to get it when we ... saw you. Marcus and Adele had invited me for drinks, remember? And he's just said you're welcome to join them. If you want to, that is. Or not. If you prefer.' I shivered, suddenly feeling how bitterly cold it was outside compared to inside End Cottage.

'You're freezing,' Sam said. 'Let's get you indoors.' He seemed to hesitate for a second as though he wasn't sure which way to go.

'I'm going to get my phone.' I pointed towards Far Cottage. 'You're welcome to come with me. And then, I don't know if you had plans, but we can come back here, where, as you saw, they're all having drinks. Or...' I let my voice trail off and turned towards Far Cottage.

'We'll get your phone, and then we'll see,' he said, falling into step beside me. 'I can't believe it's snowing.'

'Neither can I. But Tilly said it would, remember? I told you during lunch. I think.'

'Did you? I don't remember that.'

'Oh. Perhaps I didn't. It's been a very strange day.'

'You can say that again.'

'It's been a very strange day,' I repeated.

He grinned at me. 'Funny.'

'Were you really worried about me?' I shot him a look and he met it.

'Yes. Don't ask me why, but I was.'

'You're weren't just miffed because I wasn't answering your calls? Or because you thought I wasn't.'

'Miffed?' His brows furrowed but he laughed. 'No. I wasn't *miffed*. I was concerned.'

'Concerned that something had happened to me? Or concerned I might be cross with you?'

'Can we not do this right now, please?'

I stopped at the front door and turned to look him in the eye.

'I want to know. It's important.'

'Why?' His voice sounded husky and there was something in his eyes as he held my gaze, while snowflakes danced around us. He pulled the two sides of my jacket closer together to keep me warm, and then leant towards me, his body just inches from mine. 'Why is it important, Lucy? Isn't it enough to know I was concerned?'

I shook my head vigorously, the wine I'd

imbibed, clearly having an effect on me.

Several tendrils came loose from my chignon, some of which fell around my shoulders, and some, across my face. He reached out one hand and brushed them away from my eyes, his fingers touching my cheek, and sending ripples of heat to every part of me.

I swallowed and tried to maintain my breathing at a steady rate, but my heart was racing and my legs were feeling weak.

'No. Because one means you care about me, and the other means you were thinking of yourself.'

The shock in his eyes was evident and he stepped back and stared at me.

'I'm not sure what's going on here, Lucy, but as I explained today, I don't do relationships. I don't get involved. I'm not looking for anything other than a good time. If that's going to be a problem for you, say so now. We haven't seen one another for ten years. Please don't try to make this into more than it is.'

'More than it is! You were the one who wanted to have a drink to catch up. You were the one who called and asked if you could join me for lunch. You were the one who asked if I'd like to spend the week with you. Please explain how, exactly, I'm the one who is making more of this than it is.'

His brows shot together and he glared at me, and then he turned abruptly and marched away. I thought he was leaving, but he spun around and stormed back.

'Okay. Yes. That was all me. I admit that. But ... that's because something special happened between us ten years ago, and I've never felt with anyone what I felt with you back then. Seeing you again today was like ... I don't know what it was, but I do know I wanted you so badly today that it took every ounce of strength for me to walk away and leave you this afternoon. I want you, Lucy. More than I've ever wanted anyone. But that doesn't mean I love you. Or anything stupid like that. It just means I had the best sex with you I've ever had in my life. And I wanted to experience that again. I wanted to see if it would be as good this time. I wanted ... I don't know what I wanted. But I do know what I don't want. And that's this. This drama. This ... questioning. This ... whatever this is.'

'So it really is just about sex for you then? All you want is a holiday fling. A week of sex and then we go our separate ways. Just like we did ten years ago.'

'Yes. That's exactly what I want.'

'Well fine. Come in and let's have sex then. Because you know what, Sam. That's all I want from you too. Just sex, sex, and more sex. Nothing but sex. Okay?'

'Okay!'

'Fine.' I rammed the key in the lock, flung open the door, and stepped inside. 'Well? Come on then.'

He made a sort of strangled sigh and then he gave a nervous laugh and ran a hand through his hair, shaking his head as he did so.

'What the hell just happened?' His voice was calmer now.

I calmed down too. 'I have no idea. I think I've drunk far too much wine today. I should probably sleep it off.'

'That might be sensible,' he said.

I let out a sigh. 'Don't stand out there, Sam. It's snowing. Come in and I'll make some coffee.'

He hesitated. 'Are you sure?'

'I'm sure.' I walked along the hall and threw my jacket on the back of the sofa and then I kicked off my boots.

He followed me inside and his eyes scanned me from head to toe.

'What?' I asked, standing up straight. I may have pulled my shoulders back and stuck my chest out just a little.

He shook his head as he removed his leather jacket. 'Don't shout at me, but you look ... fantastic.'

I burst out laughing. 'You look pretty

good yourself.' He really did. He was now wearing smart black trousers and a white shirt.

He grinned. 'Thanks.'

'Sit,' I said. 'Unless you'd rather stand.'

'No. I'll sit.' He dropped onto the sofa and stretched out his long legs, and then he looked at me and added, 'Unless you need a hand.'

'No thanks.' I walked into the kitchen area. 'I think I can make coffee. Even if I am a little drunk.'

As it turned out, I couldn't. The coffee machine was like something from the future. On an alien planet.

'Erm. I may need your help. This machine seems to have got the better of me.'

He looked at me and grinned, before getting to his feet. 'Yep. Leave the machines to us men,' he joked.

Rather annoyingly, by the time I got the milk from the fridge, coffee was flowing into two cups.

'You'll have to show me how you did that. Or you'll have to come back tomorrow and make me my morning coffee.'

He raised one brow. 'So the night of sex, sex and nothing but sex is off then?' He was still grinning.

'I'm afraid so.'

'Damn. I was looking forward to it.'

'So was I. But I think the moment has passed, don't you?'

He shrugged. 'I guess so.' He put the cups on the counter and I added milk to both.

'Sugar?' he asked.

'Yes, honey,' I replied, then quickly added, 'Sorry. That was a joke.'

He grinned again. 'Do you take sugar?'

'No thank you. I'm sweet enough.'

'Hmm,' he said with one brow raised.'

I raised both of mine and pulled a face and then I turned to look outside. Snow was falling thicker and faster now and I could see through the sliding doors that it had already settled on the patio.

'It's really coming down. Tilly, that woman I mentioned, said we'd have a blizzard and that I might get snowed in. That we all might.'

'Really? Do you mean the Tilly who's married to Willy? Willy Trotton's wife?'

He came and stood beside me and we stood and watched the snow.

'I don't know her surname but she owns the bridal shop in town. Fairlight Brides, it's called. Ah. But you no doubt avoid shops that have even the slightest connection to weddings, don't you?'

'I do,' he said, darting a quick look at me. 'But I know Tilly, and her husband, Willy, and their dog, Billy. If Tilly said there'll be a blizzard, then there'll be a blizzard. I don't think she's ever been wrong as far as the weather is concerned.'

'Really? Wow. The Met Office should employ her.'

He grinned over the rim of his cup. 'I think they did, once upon a time. But she wanted to open a shop.'

'A *bridal* shop,' I said, rubbing it in and giving him a little nudge with my elbow.

He gave me a hard stare, and then he laughed. 'Yeah. That.' He let out a long slow sigh. 'I'd better get going before too long. Bikes are fine in all weather, generally speaking, but the lanes here can be treacherous in snow and ice, especially as they're not well lit, and the gritters won't be out for several hours, knowing the local authority. And as you said, it's really coming down now. At this rate, I might have to walk home.'

'Or stay,' I said nervously, half into my cup that hovered just below my mouth.

His head shot around and his eyes met mine as I glanced up at him. A slow smile crept across his mouth as he leant sideways a little, so that our arms were just touching.

'Or stay,' he repeated. 'But I thought we'd been over this. Sex is off the table tonight.'

'Who mentioned sex? I just said you

could stay. And it's still only eight. It might clear up before bedtime.'

He held my gaze but I could see he was holding back a laugh. 'Bedtime? Are we six?'

'You are,' I said. 'Don't be facetious. You know perfectly well what I meant by bedtime.'

'I have no idea. Enlighten me.'

'I meant later. Much later than it is now. Ten or eleven. Or midnight. I don't know what time you go to bed.' I moved my arm away from his.

He moved closer. 'It depends who I'm with. I'd happily go to bed at six with you, Lucy. Would you like me to stay?' His eyes darkened with desire.

I gave a little shrug, not wanting him to know how much I wanted him to stay.

'Would you like to stay?' I asked.

'Very much.' His gaze held mine.

'There's a second bedroom,' I said.

'Ah. I see. That's great. Then I'll stay.' He gave a small smile. 'In the second bedroom. If you're sure that's okay.'

'I'm sure. I'd worry if you drove off in this weather. Or if you walked. You might be found frozen to death or something. Better to wait until morning once the gritters have been out.'

'Yes,' he said, his eyes twinkling mischievously and his mouth twitching into a smile once again. 'Much better to wait until the morning.'

'Would you like some wine?' I walked around him to the fridge.

'Hadn't we established you've had more than enough already?'

I thumped my empty coffee cup onto the counter.

'Are you telling me how much I should, or shouldn't, drink?'

'Nope. Absolutely not. Drink as much as you like. But none for me, thanks. Even if the gritters come out, it'll still be icy tomorrow, so I need to take care.'

I opened the fridge. 'We'll be snowed in tomorrow, remember?'

'Ah yes. Hmm. Perhaps I should go, after all.'

I slammed the fridge door shut. 'Don't you want to be snowed in with me?'

He turned to face me. 'I can think of nothing I'd rather be than snowed in with you. But I'm not sure it would be wise.'

'Why not?' I folded my arms in front of my chest.

'I hate to open recent wounds, but I'm pretty sure I told you how much I wanted you. Staying in the second bed for one night is going to be hard enough, but doing so for two, is going to be impossible.'

I leant on the counter and gave him my

sexiest smile. 'And I think I told you that I wanted you too. I'll admit, I'd prefer something more than a holiday fling. I want to be in love, and be loved. I want a relationship, I'll admit that. But, like you, I had the best sex of my life ten years ago, and, like you, I'd rather like to know if it would be that good again.'

'So ... what, exactly, are you saying?'

I shrugged, and moved around the counter, leaning back against it and crossing my legs at my ankles. I reached up and pulled out my chignon, shaking my head so that my hair swung loose around my shoulders, and then I licked my lips.

'I'm saying, we're both adults. If we can be honest with one another and tell each other exactly what we both want this week, then I see no reason why we couldn't have a repeat of that wonderful week in July, ten years ago.'

He stiffened and sucked in a breath. 'Are you being serious? There's nothing I want more. I think I've made that abundantly clear. But you said you want a relationship. I can't give you that, Lucy. I could pretend, but that wouldn't be fair to either of us.'

I shook my head and twisted the knot-tie of my wrap dress around my finger.

'I don't want you to pretend.'

His eyes travelled down to my waist

where the knot-tie was the only thing holding the two sides of the front of my dress together.

'What do you want me to do, then?'

'I want you to be you. I want you to be honest with me this week. But I also need you to understand that I want to be cuddled. I want to feel special.'

'I can do that. And you are special, Lucy. I told you that ten years ago. And I'll tell you that now. Why do you think I couldn't wait to see you? I don't normally run after women, but I dropped everything today to be with you. That must tell you something.'

'Not everything. You met your dad tonight. But that's fine. I'm not complaining. I'm simply putting the record straight.'

He sighed. 'Yeah. My dad.' He shook his head. 'You wonder why I don't do relationships. I'll tell you why. My parents met when they were both eighteen. On holiday, as it happens. But they thought they were in love and they got married within a matter of weeks. Mum had me a year later, and a year after that, they were getting divorced. Mum's been married four times since then. Dad's been married three and is currently living with his most recent girlfriend. Tonight, he wanted to ask me if I thought he should get married again. Can you believe that?'

I was so surprised I couldn't reply right away, but I finally asked, 'What did you say?'

Sam looked cross and he turned away. 'I told him that if he wanted the truth, I'd say no. But that we both knew he would do it anyway. And he will. I can guarantee that before this summer is out, I'll be going to yet another one of my parents' weddings. Would you like to take a bet on how long this one will last?'

I suddenly understood why Sam didn't do relationships. At least, I thought I did. His parents were hardly an advert for a good relationship, were they? And definitely not for marriage.

I walked across to him and I slid my arms around his waist. His muscles tensed beneath my touch and he sucked in a breath, and then he spun around and swept me into his arms, kissing me with so much longing, and passion, and intensity that I thought I might faint.

Fifteen

Sam kissed me long and hard, his mouth demanding and taking, and yet also giving back. His arms were wrapped so tightly around me that I was pressed against his firm body and could hardly breathe, but he eased his hold on me as if he suddenly realised he was being too rough, too eager.

'God, I want you so badly,' he moaned as his lips moved to my neck and then back to my mouth again.

His arms loosened around me as he ran his hands up my spine and into my hair, easing my head back so that he could kiss the full length of my neck again, and then, he slowly slid one hand down my cheek, and my throat, and across my cleavage, then down to my breast and then, with a quick flick of his fingers, he undid my dress and slid his hand inside.

Now I was the one moaning how much I wanted him, and I kissed his head, his face, his mouth, and then his chest. I tugged at his shirt and pulled it open, kissing the bare skin beneath and sliding my own hands down his torso.

'Take me to bed,' I begged, not wanting to make love on the sofa, or the floor of the sitting room in this rental home, not because I would object to that, but because I wasn't sure if we might be visible if my neighbours ventured out into their gardens to play in the snow that had now settled to a depth of at least a few inches on the ground.

Sam swept me into his arms and carried me upstairs in a matter of seconds. He placed me gently on the bed, his eyes appreciating my black lace underwear, but not for long. He removed his trousers in such haste that he tumbled onto the bed and we both laughed at our mutual need for one another.

I had thought the sex we had ten years ago had been fantastic, but this was out of this world. It was as if our bodies had been made to fit together so perfectly, so precisely, so exquisitely, enabling us to attain every last ounce of pleasure.

I had joked that I wanted sex, sex, and nothing but sex, but in reality it was what we both needed. No sooner had we satisfied one another than we wanted each other again. And again. And again. Until we were both so exhausted that sleep eventually overcame us.

I had said I wanted to be cuddled, and

Sam had cuddled me. But he'd done so much more than that. He'd softly stroked my hair, and he'd gently kissed the top of my head, while I was wrapped in his arms. And when I got cramp in my leg, he massaged it tenderly until the pain vanished. He got up and made us snacks at ten p.m., and brought me a cup of tea at midnight with some biscuits. He even ran downstairs to get me a glass of water at three in the morning. And he made me coffee and toast and scrambled eggs for breakfast, and then he held me in his arms while we watched the snow falling outside the windows.

Tilly had been right. There had been a blizzard during the night. Not that Sam and I had heard it. But when Sam brought me coffee, he pulled back the curtains I'd drawn before I'd gone out last night, and I couldn't believe my eyes.

'Are we snowed in?' I asked.

'That's an understatement,' Sam replied. 'I can't see the car park across the lane, let alone my bike. It's under there somewhere but I'll have to wait until this thaws, to find it.'

'Oh no. That's not good,' I said.

He grinned at me. 'It's not all bad.' He buried his head beneath the duvet and kissed his way down my body.

Sometime later, after more coffee, we

made love again, although I had to remind myself that it wasn't love, it was sex. Great sex. Mind blowing sex. But just sex. Love didn't come into this. And yet ... I couldn't help myself.

Sam must have cared about me or he wouldn't have been so kind and thoughtful and tender, would he?

And every time he moaned my name, it was as if it had come directly from his soul.

Even the way he looked at me made me think he felt more for me than he was prepared to admit.

But I had to keep it all to myself. Until I could get a chance to discuss it in detail with Erin.

I had sent her a text at midnight while Sam was making tea.

'What a day!!!!!! Sam here. Snowing outside. Hot sex inside. He's staying the night. And tomorrow. May get snowed in. Will call you when I can. Even better than ten years ago. Details to follow. Hope all okay with you. Pleasant dreams. Soooo glad I booked this break!!!!!! Love you. Xx'

She'd sent a brief reply. 'You go girl!!!!!! Love you. Xx'

And then I'd forgotten about Erin, because Sam made love to me again, after we'd drunk our tea and eaten the biscuits.

No. Not love. I had to remember that this

had nothing to do with love.

But just like ten years before, I could already feel myself falling for Sam Worth once again.

To Sam, this was a holiday fling and in a week it would be over.

To me, this was everything. He was everything. Or he would be. If only he could feel for me, even half of what I felt for him.

When we eventually got out of bed, we made love in the shower. Finally, we managed to dress and go downstairs, but we both knew it wouldn't be that long until we were back in that bed again.

Sixteen

Snow was piled against the sliding doors, to a height of at least three feet, maybe more in places. I had never seen so much snow and I still couldn't quite believe it after the sunshine and warmth of yesterday.

'It's a good thing I brought plenty of food,' I said.

'It's a good thing I stayed,' said Sam. 'I don't think anyone is going anywhere today, not even the gritters.'

'And I don't think Melody will be out building snow people. The snow level is as high as she is tall.'

Sam grinned and walked along the hall, gingerly opening the front door and quickly closing it before the wall of snow resting against it, toppled inside.

'I think I was five when we last had this much snow,' he said. And then he let out a long and dramatic sigh. 'Oh well, I don't see any point in us staying up, do you? Especially when there's such a warm and inviting bed upstairs.'

'Sam! Shouldn't we at least make a pretence of behaving like normal people, rather than wild rabbits.'

He raised his brows. 'Why? It's not as if anyone can see us. And wild rabbits have a bad rep when really they're cute and fluffy bundles of joy.'

'Perhaps. But I need more coffee first. And you've got to show me how that machine works.'

'Come on then,' he said, taking my hand in his and leading me into the kitchen.

It took far longer than it should have, partly because we were laughing so much, and partly because we constantly stopped for kisses, but I finally got to grips with the coffee machine.

'You'll be repairing bikes next,' he said, pulling me into his arms as we waited for the coffee.

'Oh will I? Does that mean you'll be designing wedding dresses sometime soon?'

He gave me a questioning look as I ran my fingers down his chest.

'Oh, I'm sorry,' I added. 'I thought you meant we'd be tackling one another's jobs before long.'

He shook his head, but he was laughing. 'No you didn't. You just wanted to take another little dig at my commitment phobia.'

'Is it a phobia?'

'No. Phobias are fears. I'm not afraid of commitment. I simply don't believe in it. I'm just not cut out for marriage. Or long-term relationships,' Sam said with more than a hint of sadness and regret in his voice this time. 'I told you about my parents. Mum's been married four times since Dad. Dad's been married three, and is about to propose to his fourth wife-to-be. We don't do long-term relationships well in my family. Along with more than fifty percent of the population. Have you seen the divorce statistics? And your parents are divorced, so it's not just mine, and half the world, who couldn't make marriage work.'

'But Mum has remarried again. And Chris, her new husband, is the love of her life. Don't you believe there's someone out there for each of us?'

He shook his head again and eased me away from him, walking towards the fridge as he spoke.

'Nope. That's the stuff of fairytales, in my opinion. Life isn't a fairytale, Lucy.'

'I know that,' I said, taking the milk from him as he reached out for the cups. 'But we have to believe in something or what's the point? I do believe in love and marriage. I believe there's someone out there I could happily spend the rest of my life with. Raise a family with. Share my good times and bad times with. Don't you want that? Wouldn't you like to have someone special in your life?'

He narrowed his eyes as he looked at me, a deep crease forming between his brows.

'I do have someone special in my life,' he finally said. 'And she's standing right beside me.'

'Oh Sam!' My heart soared in my chest, but it soon came crashing to the ground.

'But that doesn't mean I'm about to have a relationship. People come and go in our lives. It's important to enjoy times like this, and then move on to the next experience.'

'Oh, Sam,' I sighed. 'For a moment there I thought there was hope.'

He tensed visibly and I realised this was dangerous ground.

'What did you do with the biscuits?' I quickly added.

'Biscuits? Oh. From last night. They're in that cupboard.'

He nodded towards the end cupboard of the row and then he went and got them. I didn't want a biscuit, but it was the first thing that had popped into my head, so I took one, and my coffee, and I went and sat on the sofa.

Sam came and sat beside me, bringing his own coffee with him, together with the packet of biscuits which he placed on the coffee table as I stared out at the wall of white.

'Are we okay?' he asked.

'Yes. We're ... great. Aren't we?'

He nodded. 'Yep. We're great.'

It was only then that I realised there were flames dancing behind the glass door of the wood burner.

'When did you light that?' I asked, pointing towards it.

'When I made breakfast,' he said.

'Wow. You're handy to have around.' I smiled at him.

'All part of the service.' He smiled back.

'Do you need me to give you a review or something? Because you'll get five stars from me if so.'

'Only five? I was hoping I had excelled.'

'Oh you have. Five out of five is only for those who excel. Okay, but six is as high as I'll go. And no one ever gets a six from me. Or a five, for that matter, so you should be as pleased as punch.'

He turned to look me directly in the eye. 'No one? Ever?'

'Nope.'

'Not even Ted?'

I'd completely forgotten about Ted, as awful as that seems.

'Not even Ted. Although he did come close.'

'But ... he wasn't the one. That special

someone you believe is out there for you. The one you could happily spend the rest of your life with. Raise a family with. Share your good times and bad times with.'

'No. He wasn't.'

'But ... you genuinely believe that? That's really what you want?'

'Absolutely. I want to love and be loved. I told you that. I want someone who makes my heart soar and my entire body tingle. Someone who wants me and needs me so badly that they can't stop thinking about me. Someone who looks at me as if I'm the most beautiful woman in the world.'

'You are, Lucy. I mean, I think you're beautiful. And ... part of that other stuff applies to me. I think I made that clear last night. It's just ... the love thing I can't do. And the lifetime commitment I can't give you.'

'Ah, so close and yet so far. Was that the doorbell?'

Sam was looking at me so intensely but the chime of the bell made him turn his head towards the front door.

'Shall I?' he asked.

'Please do,' I replied. 'You need to keep that five-star rating.'

'Six,' he said, leaning over to give me a quick kiss before he stood up. 'You gave me six, remember? And, as it happens, you're a six too.'

'Obviously!' My heart did a little leap yet again, as Sam strolled towards the front door.

'Good morning.' Marcus sounded pleased to see Sam, but not entirely surprised.

'Good morning to you,' said Sam, and then he called out to me, 'Lucy. Marcus has freed us from our golden prison. He's removed the wall of snow. And, it seems, he's carved a path to this front door and along the lane to his.'

I got up and went to greet him.

'Crikey, Marcus! How on earth did you do that? Good morning, by the way.'

Marcus laughed. 'I've got skills,' he joked. 'And tools.'

'And helpers,' said Alec, appearing beside him. 'Good morning, Lucy.' He grinned at Sam knowingly, and Sam smiled back. 'And Sam. Noelle wants to know if you need anything.'

'As does Adele,' said Marcus, also grinning as if they were all in on some joke.

I hoped I wasn't the joke.

'Thank you both,' I said. 'And please thank Adele and Noelle, but I'm fine. I've got everything I need.' And then I couldn't help myself. I slipped my arm through Sam's and gave them all my sexiest smile. 'And *everything* I could possibly want. Sam's making sure of that.'

All three of them looked at me and then Alec and Marcus looked at Sam.

'What a good thing you arrived when you did,' Marcus said.

'Perfect timing,' said Alec.

'I thought so,' said Sam. 'Although I'm not sure when I'll see my bike again. I may need to borrow some tools, Marcus, and possibly some man-power to dig it out. But not today. Obviously.'

'Obviously not,' said Marcus. 'Right. We'll leave you to it. Just give me a shout when you want to search for your bike.'

'I don't think I'll be going to work on Monday,' said Alec. 'Unless there's another drastic change in the weather. So I can give you a hand as well. Keep warm,' he added, with an even bigger grin.

'Count on it,' I said. 'I hope Melody gets a chance to build her snow people.'

'She's checking the snow depth every half hour. Do you want us to give you a call when the fun's about to start? Or do you have other plans?'

Sam and I exchanged glances and smiles.

'Making snow people sounds like fun, so yes please,' I said.

'And getting warm in front of a roaring fire afterwards, sounds even better,' Sam said. 'So I'm in.'

'We'll just have to find a way to occupy ourselves until then,' I teased.

'We've got Monopoly,' said Alec, and then laughed. 'I'm leaving. Good bye for now. Have fun.'

'I'm up for Monopoly,' said Marcus. 'And I'm sure Adele will be too. Although she did say she might bake some of her delicious chocolate brownies.'

'Melody would love to help,' said Alec.

'Good bye to you both,' said Sam, laughing as he closed the front door.

I could hear Marcus and Alec laughing as they walked away and I was just about to turn and walk back to the sofa when Sam pulled me into his arms.

'What game could we play, I wonder?' he said, his eyes darkening with desire.

'Hmm. Let me think.' I tapped my fingers against my lips and then trailed them down the front of my dress. 'Nope. Nothing comes to me right away.'

'Oh doesn't it?' That gorgeous smile of his lit up his face and his eyes. 'Well, I have a few ideas.'

He swept me up in his arms once again and carried me back to the bedroom.

Seventeen

'I like being snowed in with you,' Sam said two hours later as I lay wrapped in his arms. 'We should do this again.'

'We should. I'll pencil it in for ten years' time.'

He shifted his position to throw me a look. 'I may not like commitment, Lucy, but I'd be happy to commit to that. Or even to two years. Or ... less. Possibly.'

'Let's see how the rest of this week goes,' I said, trying to play it cool and avoiding his eyes after the last two hours of incredible sex. I was so close to blurting out the words, 'I love you, Sam,' that it frightened me.

He lifted me from him and tilted my chin so that he could look me in the eye.

'Have I done something wrong? Or said something I shouldn't have?' There was genuine concern in his eyes.

'No! You've been ... great. Better than great. You've been ... perfect. But ... we've already had one blazing row. We might have more before the week is out.'

'Why would we? We understand each other much better now, don't you think? I was a jerk yesterday. I'll admit that. But I didn't want to lie to you. Or to lead you on. Or make you think this might lead to something I knew it wouldn't. It couldn't.'

'Yes. I think we've established what this won't lead to. All I meant was, despite the sex being wonderful and working perfectly between us, we don't really know one another, do we?'

'Don't we? I feel like we do. I feel as if I've known you all my life.' He laughed. 'And I have known you for ten years.'

'No. You knew me for one week, ten years ago. And now you've known me for one day.'

'Is that ... is that how you really feel? That you hardly know me?'

'Please don't be cross,' I soothed, reaching out and stroking his cheek.

He took my hand in his and kissed it. 'I'm not cross. I'm ... a little sad, that's all. Sad that you feel that way. I feel I know you inside and out.'

I smiled seductively. 'You certainly know me ... intimately after last night and today.'

He pulled me in for a kiss.

Afterwards, I eased myself away.

'To continue. There are lots of things you

don't know about me, Sam. For example. You don't know my favourite colour.'

'It's red. And purple. You like them both.'

'Oh!' His correct response startled me. 'Yours is black. And dark blue is a close second.'

He smiled. 'You see. We do know one another.'

'Okay. Favourite song?'

He tutted. 'Oh come on, Lucy. That's not fair. I know what it was ten years ago. Jason Derulo's *Want to Want Me*.'

'Yes! It was your favourite too.'

He nodded. 'It was. Now it's anything by Sam Fender. I haven't really been listening to much music lately.'

'I like his stuff too,' I said, astonished that we still appeared to have similar tastes. 'But like you. I haven't been listening to music as much as I normally would.'

'Favourite person to kiss?' Sam asked before pulling me to him again. 'If it's not me, I don't want to know.'

'Oh it's you, Sam. It's definitely you.'

Eighteen

The snow had melted enough for us all to go outside by around three-thirty, but it was still deep, although the handlebars of Sam's bike were just visible, poking through the snow like dark snowdrops, or crocuses.

The top bar of the handrail on the wooden bridge was also visible although the bridge itself was still buried, as was Midwinter Brook, but a wide dip that followed the course of the brook showed where it ran.

The clouds were heavy, threatening more snow to come and the air was cold, clear and crisp but it wouldn't be that long until it was dark.

I'd brought my winter coat as well as my jacket, so I wore that now and we went outside to build snow people with Melody, and the rest of our neighbours.

We teamed up. Men against women. Naturally the men cheated, but we women still won, building our snow person first.

'There were four of you,' Sam grumbled, but he was laughing.

'Three and a half,' said Melody, 'Because I'm much smaller than you and I could only just reach to put the snow person's hat on his head.'

'Don't be a bad loser as well as a cheat,' I said.

I threw a snowball at Sam, which caused a male against female snowball fight. We won that too, although this time we were the ones who cheated, by pretending that Noelle was hurt, and then pelting the guys with all the snowballs Adele, Melody and I had secretly made while they were tending to Noelle's 'injuries'. None of which she had.

After that, we played, jumping the brook. Well the men did. We women sat on the garden chairs that Marcus and Alec, with Sam's help, had brought around from their gardens, and we drank hot chocolate, sitting in front of the firepit that Marcus and the guys had also dragged around to the common ground between the cottages and the brook.

Adele brought out the chocolate brownies she, Noelle and Melody had made that morning, and we stuffed our faces while the men did 'manly' stuff. Otherwise known as doing the most ridiculous and possibly dangerous things they could whilst competing against one another.

'Remember we're snowed in up here, and the hospital is miles away,' I said, when Sam caught his foot on the rail of the bridge while leaping over it. He almost fell on his face but he managed to safe himself and landed on his feet to everyone's surprise, including his. The others didn't attempt it, so Sam won that particular, trial.

'Don't you just love all these testosterone-driven antics?' said Noelle.

'I love some of them,' I said, thinking about last night and this morning.

'Me too,' said Adele.

'What's testerone?' Melody asked, mispronouncing it.

'Testosterone,' Noelle corrected, giving a small cough. 'Ask your dad. He'll explain it far better than we could.'

'Are you getting cold?' Sam asked, suddenly dashing over, crouching in front of me, and planting a quick kiss on my lips.

I'm not sure who was most surprised. Him, me, or the neighbours.

'Sorry,' he said, standing up abruptly. 'I think the cold is getting to me.'

'That's fine,' I said, grinning as I could see from the corner of my eye that Noelle was mouthing the word, 'testosterone'. 'But it is getting chilly. It's so nice out here though, I don't want to go inside just yet.'

'We've got blankets, said Adele.

'And throws,' said Noelle.

'We'll get them,' Alec, Marcus, and even Sam, offered.

A few minutes later, the men had dragged more chairs around, made two large flasks of hot chocolate, brought out a bottle of brandy, a pile of blankets and several throws, and more wood for the firepit.

We all sat drinking, chatting, and laughing until the sun, that had made a brief appearance just before it set, finally disappeared, and the streetlamps burst into life, just as the temperature seemed to plummet.

'It's freezing,' Noelle said. 'I think we should take this inside.'

'Good idea,' said Adele.

'We need to eat,' said Sam. 'We ... missed lunch.'

All eyes turned to us as we all stood up.

'I can cook,' Marcus offered.

'Do you want a medal?' Alec teased.

'I meant, I'll cook supper for us all, if you like.'

Sam met my eyes and I smiled and nodded. He nodded too.

'That sounds great, Marcus,' Sam said. 'If you're sure you don't mind.'

'Not at all.'

'Marcus loves to cook,' said Adele.

'Alec and I will take the furniture back,' said Sam.

'We'll leave the firepit to cool though,' suggested Alec.

'I can help prep veg,' I said. 'Or help with anything else. Oh. But I do need to give my best friend, Erin a quick call, if that's okay. She texted me earlier and I haven't got back to her.'

Sam gave me an odd look but then he smiled and piled up the chairs.

'We'll see you when you've done that,' said Adele. 'Don't bother with the bell. We'll leave the door on the latch.'

They all headed towards End Cottage, Melody skipping through the snow and then dropping on the ground to make a snow angel, while I went to Far Cottage, poured myself a quick glass of wine, and phoned Erin.

'So you're still alive then? I was about to phone the murder squad. Although I don't think Fairlight Bay has one.' She laughed.

'Sorry! Oh Erin, I've got so much to tell you, I don't know where to start.'

I filled her in on everything. The way Sam had turned up unexpectedly, the great sex, the cuddles, the lovely little gestures that made me believe Sam might have feelings for me, however deeply they might be hidden, and the blizzard.

'It's been snowing here too,' she said. 'Not as bad as there, but it's settled. So does that mean he's staying until it thaws?'

'He's staying another night. We're going to have supper at End Cottage. That's where Adele and Marcus live. After that, who knows? But I hope he stays all week. I can't get enough of him, Erin. And I know I said I would try to stay cool, but I'm already half in love with him again.'

'Tell me something I don't know.' She let out a sigh. 'I just hope you can get over him this time.'

'Me too,' I said. 'I wish I lived in Fairlight Bay.'

'I'm glad you don't. I'd miss you.'

'There's a police force here too. And the sea air would do you good.'

She laughed loudly. 'Are you seriously trying to convince me that we should both move down to the seaside? What about your mum and Chris?'

'It's only about sixty miles or so. They could come and visit and I could nip back home every other week or so.'

'So that's a yes then?'

'Would it ... would it be such a bad idea?'

'If Sam doesn't want a relationship with you, yes it would. A horrible idea. Your worst idea ever.'

'But what if he does? I mean, if I lived

here and he still wanted me as much as he seems to want me, then surely...?'

'Oh don't ask me, Lucy! You need to ask him how he'd feel about that. Because believe me. It's much, much harder to get over someone when there's a chance you'll see them every day. And it's taken you ten years without seeing him, so imagine the hell it'd be to see him with other women. I can't believe you're considering this.'

'I'm not! Not really. At least, I wasn't. The idea has only just come to me. But you're right. It's dumb. And although I could design wedding dresses from anywhere, Mum needs help at the shop. Sorry. Forget I said anything about moving down to Fairlight Bay.'

'It would be good to see the place,' she said. 'But as for moving. I don't think so, do you? Okay. Let's change the subject.'

'What have you been up to?' I asked.

'Working. Making the streets safe. Eating my own bodyweight in food from the staff canteen. My life is so exciting I can hardly bear it. And I'm on shift again soon. Call me when you can. I need updates.'

'Will do. Stay safe.'

'Always. Love you.'

'Love you too.'

I rang off and sat on the sofa staring out at the garden still covered in a blanket of snow.

Would moving to Fairlight Bay really be such a dumb idea?

Nineteen

Supper at End Cottage was a lively and entertaining affair, and I felt as if Sam and I were a real couple. I really liked all my neighbours, and I found myself wishing, once again, that I lived in Fairlight Bay. I loved Erin with all my heart, but I knew that I could also be good friends with Noelle and Alec, and Adele and Marcus. As could Erin, if she moved here too.

Sam and I finally returned to Far Cottage around ten p.m., and walked with Noelle to Middle Cottage, Alec having left a little after nine-thirty to get Melody to bed.

I hadn't realised he and Noelle had only been dating since last December, although I think Adele might have mentioned it. I also discovered Melody was his child and that he was a widower, who didn't actually live with Noelle, but who had a home of his own down in Fairlight Bay. From what I had gleaned during supper, he and Melody spent half the week in Middle Cottage, and then Noelle joined them for the remainder of the week at Alec's home.

I also discovered that Adele and Marcus had a rather strange and dramatic history. He had been married to a nasty woman who had cheated on him with his best friend, who at the time lived in Noelle's cottage. Marcus' ex-wife had moved in with Marcus' former best friend, and then they'd moved away together. Just last Christmas the pair got married. Adele and Marcus hadn't spoken to one another for years, thanks to Marcus' ex-wife. But last December, Noelle had helped bring Adele and Marcus together. And now they were inseparable, and deeply in love. As were Alec and Noelle, it seemed.

'Perhaps I shouldn't bring this up,' I said, as Sam and I walked into Far Cottage and closed the door behind us, 'but did you hear that Alec's first love had died, and now he's found his second? And Marcus picked the wrong woman first, but now he's found the right one? So I understand your point about the divorce rate and all that. But surely you can see mine, about there being someone special for everyone? Noelle and Alec found each other, as did Adele and Marcus.'

Sam met my eyes after helping me off with my coat and we stood facing one another in the hall.

'You're assuming that Alec and Noelle,

163

and Adele and Marcus will stay together. They might not.'

I raised my brows in disbelief and my mouth fell open.

'Are you serious? Didn't you see how deeply in love each couple is?'

'I saw two couples who seem to be happy with each other. At the moment. But they've only been couples since December. Talk to me again when they've been together for years.'

'You're unbelievable! How can you ignore the fact they're so in love. Deeply in love. They were clearly made for one another.'

'Says you.' He turned and walked into the kitchen and I followed. 'We've had a lovely evening, Lucy. Let's not ruin it by disagreeing.' He reached out for me but I held back. He let out a long sigh and ran a hand through his hair. 'You're going to do this, aren't you?'

'Do what? Prove you wrong?'

'Prove me right. I really like you, Lucy, and that week we spent together ten years ago was the best week of my life. I told you that. And this week so far has, if anything, only been better. But I can't give you what you want. I can't have a relationship with you. It would break us both. It would ruin this. Ruin our memories. What we had then was special. What we have had over the last two days has been more so. It will stay with me forever. I want to spend the rest of this week with you. I really do. Doing what we've been doing. Enjoying each other and having a good time. But I can't give you more than that. And I can't keep having this argument about love, and about there being just one special person for each of us. You believe that. I don't. Can't we just agree to disagree? I can't give you more. I can't make you promises. I can't be the man you want me to be. I can't get into some sort of relationship with you. Especially not a long distance one. I don't want a relationship. Why can't you just let me be me? I can't be anyone else. I'm not prepared to live a lie. Not even for you.'

I stared at him in silence, unable to think of anything to say. Unable to stop the pain searing through me. I shouldn't have drunk so much wine during supper. I shouldn't have started this conversation. This argument as he called it.

He let out another sigh. 'I'll sleep in the other room tonight. And I'll leave in the morning. The snow should be passable by then. I'm sorry it had to end like this, Lucy. I truly am. I was really looking forward to this week and... what's the point? I've said all I can possibly say.'

I ran up the stairs and slammed the

bedroom door behind me, collapsing onto the bed in a heap.

Why had I been so stupid? He'd made his position clear from the start. Several times, in fact.

Why couldn't I just enjoy what we had?

Why did I have to keep pushing him for more, even though I knew he couldn't give it? Wouldn't give it.

Even though I knew he didn't love me, why did I keep wishing and hoping that he would?

Twenty

'Are you okay?' Sam asked through the closed door, tapping gently on the wood just a few minutes later. 'I ... I don't want to leave things like this, Lucy. I don't want to hurt you. I ... I just wish you could see things from my point of view.'

Like the fool that I was, I ran to the door, flung it open, and threw myself into his arms. I was more than a little relieved when he held me tightly and I heard a small sigh of something akin to relief, escape him.

'I'm so sorry, Sam. Please forgive me. I don't know why I keep doing this. You've made your position clear. And you're right. Of course you are. We should simply agree to disagree. I won't mention love, or finding the one, or anything like that again. I want to spend this week with you as much as you want to spend it with me. Let's just do that, can we? Let's forget this stupid conversation happened and pretend we've just walked in.'

He stroked my hair and kissed the top of

my head.

'I can do that, Lucy. If you can.'

I looked up into his eyes. 'I can, Sam. I can.'

And it seemed, I could. Or at least I could pretend I could.

We made love – sorry, we had sex that night as if nothing had happened. And the following day we sat and talked and cooked and laughed and joked about anything and everything. Except relationships and love and happy ever after.

We spent time with our neighbours who didn't notice anything was different between Sam and me.

But I knew something was. And it hurt like hell.

Obviously, when I told Erin, she was cross with me.

'You need to walk away,' she said, 'before your heart gets broken beyond repair. Sam is not the man for you. I know you think he is, but he clearly isn't.'

'He is, Erin. I know he is. If I can't have Sam, I don't want anyone.'

'You need help,' she said. 'Seriously. Stop being such a bloody drama queen. This isn't like you, Lucy. I don't know what's happened to you.'

'I know you're right. I think … I think it's the fact that things didn't work out with me and Ted that's sort of tipped me over the edge, somehow. It's not about Ted. It's about me. I think I've been drifting. When I was at uni, I had such dreams of being a brilliant, wedding dress designer. And then Mum and Dad split up and I joined Mum in the shop as soon as she took over the lease. Don't get me wrong, I love it. I love the shop. I love the online business. But I think I put my own dreams on hold. I did the same with Ted, in a way. I knew things weren't going well, but what did I do? Book a romantic break to try to save the relationship. Every time a bride comes into the shop, I feel more desperate, as if my dream of finding my own true love, of having kids, and a happy ever after, is slipping further and further away. Just like my dream of being a wedding dress designer has.'

'So do something about it. Design more wedding dresses. Start your own bridal shop and design business, separate from your mum's but in tandem. Open a branch somewhere. Even in Fairlight Bay if you really must. But do something! Don't let your dreams slip away. And as for finding the one, as I said, once you're back we'll concentrate on that. Sam is not the only man in the world you will ever love. I can't believe that. Life sucks sometimes, I know, but it wouldn't be that cruel. But why do you feel you need a man so badly, anyway? You can be a single mum if you want kids. You can have a family consisting of friends, and your mum and Chris, and me of course. You don't need to find just one man to make your life complete. To make your dreams come true.'

'I know. You're right of course. I realise that. And yet, I always saw myself with a husband and a family.'

'You always saw yourself with Sam Worth, is what you really mean, isn't it? But that might be a nightmare, rather than a dream. How are things on that front?'

'They're ... great. The sex is brilliant. We're having a good time. And we're enjoying ourselves. There's just that constant tiny niggle and it simply won't stop.'

'Be careful, Lucy. Sometimes it's better if we don't get what we wish for.'

'And sometimes, what we wish for, we can't have. Tell me about you. I'm sick of talking about me.'

Twenty-one

What are you supposed to do when you're with someone you're just having sex with, and yet Valentine's Day is looming? Do you simply ignore it, and carry on regardless? Or do you buy a card, a gift, and arrange something special, and pretend you're a couple, even though you're not?

I decided the best thing to do was to broach the subject with Sam.

'It's Valentine's Day on Friday,' I said, and I saw Sam stiffen immediately, as though bracing himself for impact, from some sort of emotional missile.

'Is it?' He continued buttering the toast he'd made as if I'd said it was a plain old Tuesday or something.

'It is. And without causing a row or anything, I was wondering if we should, sort of, celebrate it in some way. We are lovers, after all, even if we're not actually, in love.'

Well, one of us wasn't but I'd promised not to bring that up, so I kept silent on that score.

He looked me in the eye and he seemed to scan my face and possibly my thoughts.

'We could do that. What did you have in mind?'

'Oh!' I was so surprised he'd agreed that it threw me off track. 'I don't know. I hadn't given it any thought. Other than I knew it was this Friday. We could exchange cards. Funny cards, obviously, because we're not in love, are we?'

His eyes scanned my face.

'No, Lucy. We're not.'

'Right. So jokey cards. And perhaps a silly little fun gift?'

His brows knit together but then he nodded.

'I can do that.'

'Great!'

'And ... what about if I cooked something special. Just for fun. Or we could go out to a restaurant or something.'

'Not a restaurant. No. That's for people who believe they are genuinely in love. We don't believe that, do we, Lucy?' He was shaking his head as if he felt he needed to direct my reaction.

'In love? Us!' Pah! Of course not. No. I agree. Let's just have a lovely meal here then. And a bottle of champers or something.'

He frowned suddenly. 'You're not

expecting red roses or anything, are you?'

'Ooh! That would be lovely. But no. Don't worry. I'm not expecting flowers of any variety.'

'Or chocolates?'

'Nope.'

'Or perfume?'

'Na-huh. Nothing. Just two ... friends, enjoying each other's company and a nice meal and some champagne and then, hopefully, the best sex of our lives. Just to round the week off, you understand?'

He almost choked on the bite of toast he'd just put in his mouth.

'No pressure then?'

'None whatsoever. Are we agreed?'

'I'll do my best. But I'm not sure how I'll perform under pressure. The best sex of our lives is a lot. We've had some pretty fantastic sex this week, haven't we?'

'Yeah. It's been good.'

'Good? Just good? Not great?'

'Yeah. Some of it was great. But you know how it is. When couples are in love, everything is rosy. Even bad sex. But when it's just about sex, the expectations are so much higher, don't you think? Or maybe that's just me.'

'Are you saying you have complaints about my performance?'

'No! Well. Not complaints, exactly.'

'But you feel I could improve in some way?'

'We can all improve, Sam. No one is perfect. Don't worry though. I'm not keeping score. And after Friday, we'll be going our separate ways. Probably for another ten years. Or so.'

He dropped his slice of toast and pulled me into his arms, staring directly into my eyes.

'Tell me what I can do to make the sex the best you've ever had. Tell me what you need.'

'Oh. Erm. I'm not really sure. I mean, it's been great. Don't get me wrong. But I have felt, on occasion, that something has been … lacking. But perhaps that's how it always feels unless the participants are truly in love.'

'Then … what are you saying? That to make the sex fantastic we'd need to be in love?' Or to believe we are?'

'Hmm. I'm not sure. But yes. I think being in love with the person you're having sex with definitely helps. It is called, making love after all. Obviously, we're not in love, are we? So I suppose the sex we've been having is the best it is going to get. Ah well. C'est la vie, and all that. What would you like to eat?' I eased myself out of his embrace.

'Eat? Sorry? What? When?'

'On Valentine's Day, Sam.'

'Oh. I don't really care.'

'No. And that's probably why the sex isn't as great as it could be, if you did. The snow's almost melted, so I'm going to venture out to the shops.'

I knew Sam would come after me, and he did.

'Are you saying you think things could be better between us, sexually, I mean?'

'Uh-huh. Don't you?'

He fell into step beside me. 'I didn't. No. But maybe now I do. What do you suggest we do to ... improve things? I thought it was ... pretty fantastic.'

'Yes. Men always do. Women, you'll find, have higher expectations.'

'You're saying you expected more from me? What more could I do?'

'I don't know, Sam. Maybe, get in touch with your feelings, or something. Or pretend you're in love with me. Truly in love with me. Perhaps that might help. I'll leave that up to you.'

He stopped in his tracks and I knew his jaw had dropped open because I took a surreptitious glance at him as I walked away, taking extra care not to slip on the remaining snow and ice.

Twenty-two

I awoke to sunshine on Friday morning – Valentine's Day – and to breakfast in bed, consisting of a glass of champagne, freshly squeezed orange juice, poached eggs, mushrooms, bacon, and tomatoes, together with toast and marmalade, delivered on a faux silver tray, with a single red rose in a bud vase, a card, and a beautifully wrapped gift. Sam had gone above and beyond, and for one brief moment, when he smiled at me and bent down to kiss me, I actually believed he loved me.

'This is a first for me,' he said, 'so I hope it's okay. I need to pop into town to my showroom this morning, but I'll be back as soon as I can and we'll do something special. It's a beautiful day, so maybe we could go for a ride, or something? Anyway, enjoy your breakfast and I'll see you soon.'

'Thank you,' I called after him. 'I'll give you your card and present later then, shall I?'

'Yeah,' he called back. 'That's fine.'

Well this was a great start to Valentine's Day. The breakfast in bed was lovely, but surely he could've stayed and enjoyed it with me?

The card, to my surprise was fairly romantic. It had two cherubs on the front, shooting arrows at one another. Maybe that wasn't so romantic after all. Inside it read, 'Be My Valentine' and he had signed it simply, 'Sam'. He had added one kiss though, so that was something.

The gift however, was a complete surprise. It was a silver, heart-shaped locket, and inside sat a photo we had taken together in a photo booth on Fairlight Bay pier just the day before. I had wondered why he was so adamant about having our photos taken in that booth and whether or not he remembered we'd had our photos taken there before. Now I had my answer. Alongside the photo in the locket was another photo of us both, taken ten years earlier, in the same photo booth.

I was utterly astonished. I had kept my copies of the photos we'd had taken that day all those years ago. I had no idea Sam had kept his copies too.

I put the necklace on, vowing never to take it off again. Except to shower, and maybe before I went to sleep.

I'd bought Sam a dancing heart, that did

little back-flips when you wound the spring. Not quite as romantic. But I hadn't expected a real gift from him. Just a jokey token. This was a complete surprise.

And that wasn't the only surprise I was to receive. Except the next one wasn't from Sam.

I had seen the florist's van pull up in the car park opposite – because I was looking out for Sam's return. It was just my luck that he drove up on his bike, as the florist was leaving the front door, having delivered a massive bouquet of two dozen red roses ... from Ted.

I'd decided earlier that morning – before I'd opened the gift from Sam – that although I might never love anyone as much as I loved Sam, if I could find someone like Ted, I might be able to be relatively happy.

I wanted a home, a family, a wedding.

Sam would never give me those things. He'd made that abundantly clear.

But someone like Ted might. And now, having read the rather gushingly romantic card accompanying the roses, before I had seen Sam return, it seemed Ted wanted to give me those things. He'd realised how much he'd missed me. And how much he cared about me. And the note with the card informed me that, on his return from Portugal, we would go out to dinner where he intended to ask me a very particular question. I was fairly certain it wasn't about my taxes.

I considered trying to hide the roses, but Sam had clearly seen the florist, and also the bouquet I was holding at the door. I could hide the note, but what was the point? Sam wouldn't care. So instead, I went back inside, leaving the door ajar for Sam to enter, and I put the roses in a vase and placed the vase on the counter with the gushing card beside it.

Sam didn't look happy.

'Were those flowers for you?' he asked, as soon as he stepped inside the front door. 'Ah. I see they were.'

'They're from Ted,' I said, seeing no benefit in lying. 'He's had a change of heart and he wants us to have dinner when he returns from Portugal. He says he has something in particular to ask me.'

'Oh does he?' Sam said, sounding none too pleased.

'I love this locket,' I said, holding out the heart shaped locket Sam had bought me. 'And I can't believe you kept those photos from all those years ago.'

He furrowed his brows, and glared at the massive display of red roses.

'I assume you didn't.'

'I did. I can't believe you kept yours.'

'Why wouldn't I?' He shrugged, still

glaring at the roses as if they might attack him any second.

'Because it's romantic. And you don't believe in love and all that stuff.'

'I didn't say I didn't believe in love, exactly. I said it doesn't last. My parents, and even yours are proof of that. Along with thousands of others who've got divorced. Okay. Maybe I did say I didn't believe in it. So, Ted wants you back, does he?'

'It would seem so.'

'And?'

'And what?'

'Will you go back to him?'

I shrugged. 'I honestly don't know. We get on well. And I know he believes in love and marriage and kids and all that. But...'

'But what?'

I looked him in the eye. 'I don't love him. Not in the way you should love the man you intend to marry.'

'You intend to marry him?' He looked distraught. 'Why in God's name would you do that?'

'Because I want a husband, and a home, and a family, and a pet dog, and cat, and everything else that goes with it. I want to love and be loved. I want someone special in my life.'

'You ... you don't have to get married to have those things.'

'Maybe not. But that's what I want.'

'I ... I don't know what to say.'

'There's nothing to say, is there? You don't love me, do you? You've made that abundantly clear.'

'What if I did? Love you, I mean.'

I looked him in the eye wondering what was happening.

'But you don't, do you?'

'What if I did?'

'But you don't. Or are you saying that you think you might?

He glared at the roses again.

'Do I have to buy two dozen red roses to show you that I do?'

My heart did a little leap.

'No. You just have to tell me. You simply have to say the words.'

'The words, I ... love you?'

'Yes. But without the inflection on the end. It needs to be a statement, not a question.'

He sucked in a breath and ran a hand through his hair.

'I've been to see Dad. And also, Mum.'

'Have you? That's ... nice.'

He rested his hands on the back of a chair and looked me in the eye.

'You know my parents have been married and divorced more times and to more people than most people move home.

Well, I didn't want that. I didn't want endless broken families, in my life. So I decided I'd never get married. No matter what. But Dad has often told me I was missing out on something that could be wonderful. Not that any of his, or Mum's marriages, have been that, but Dad said at least they've both tried to find happiness. He told me today that I run from happiness. Do you think I do that?'

'I think it's possible that you do, yes.'

'Hmm. Mum says I do too. Anyway, Dad said it was like someone having parents who are serial killers. He asked me if I thought that meant their child would automatically be a serial killer too? I had to agree that it didn't. He told me that just because he and my mum aren't good at relationships, it didn't follow that I would be bad at them as well. Unless I thought I was. That was a sort of self-fulfilling prophecy. "You're your own man, Sam," he said. "You can be whatever you want to be and do whatever you want to do." He also told me that he'd never had feelings for any woman that were anything like the feelings I have for you, Lucy. And Mum has never felt that way about any man, so he said. I asked her about that afterwards, and she agreed with Dad. "Believe me, son," she said, "if either of us had felt even half of what you say you feel for Lucy, we would have both run, not walked that person down the aisle. You'd be a fool to give up on a love like that just because of some irrational fear that it might not last or that you're not worthy." And then she told me to stop being such a total jerk and to come and tell you how I felt. So here I am, Lucy. Except, I didn't expect to have competition. And I only gave you one red rose. Not a whole bunch of the damn things.'

I wasn't sure I'd heard him correctly, at first.

'You don't have competition, believe me. But ... are you saying what I think you're saying?'

He furrowed his brow. 'If you think I'm telling you, in a rather long-winded and roundabout way, that I love you, then yes. I am. Is that what you think I said?'

I nodded. 'Uh-huh.'

'Okay then. At least we're on the same page. Unless ... you don't love me, that is. But you do. Don't you?'

I laughed at that.

'You know I do, you utter imbecile.'

'Imbecile? I thought I did that rather well. You have no idea how hard that was for me to say. I had to get it all out at once or I might not have said any of it. I'm not used to doing this. Or to saying this stuff. But just to make it clear and for the avoidance of all doubt. I love you, Lucy. I've always loved you.'

And only you. I just didn't want us to end up like Mum and Dad. But this week has made me realise that my life is so much better with you in it than out of it. So I want you in it for ever from now on. I want to spend the rest of my life making you happy. I want to be the man I know you want me to be. The man *I* want to be. The man you deserve. Because I want to be with you more than I've ever wanted anything in my life.'

'Oh, Sam,' I said, running to him and throwing myself into his arms. 'I love you, Sam. Just the way you are. I've always loved you.'

'Well,' he said. 'That wasn't as hard as I thought it was going to be. I should tell you I love you more often.'

'That would be lovely,' I said. 'But ... actually. There's something I need to tell you, Sam. Something that might change the way you feel about me.'

He looked both sceptical and concerned. 'Okay. But nothing will change the way I feel about you, Lucy, so don't worry about that. If it's something from your past, I don't care. If it's something in your present or your future, we will deal with it together, whatever it is.'

I took a deep breath. 'I have aerophobia,' I said. Not wanting to keep anything from him. 'That's a fear of flying.'

He let out a huge sigh of relief and

beamed at me as he pulled me back into his arms.

'Oh god, Lucy. I thought you were going to tell me something dreadful.'

I revelled in his embrace, but then I eased myself away and looked into his eyes.

'I don't think you understand, Sam. Okay, it's not a serious illness or anything like that, but it's a condition that causes a severe reaction and means my travel options are restricted. I've never been on a plane. Just the thought of it brings me out in a cold sweat.' My words were tumbling out and although Sam's mouth was opening and closing, I didn't give him the chance to speak. 'The first time I tried to get on a plane I had severe chest pains, dizziness, and nausea. I couldn't breathe and I thought I'd either be sick or pass out at any minute. And that was just in the airport. I keep telling myself it's an irrational fear, but I can't help it. I went to see a specialist but that didn't work. I even tried hypnotherapy. The next time I went to an airport, I made it as far as the check-in desk but I was sweating and trembling, and I wanted to scream. Then the nausea, rapid heartbeat and dizziness kicked in, and even Usain Bolt would've had a hard time catching up with me, I ran out of that place so fast. I'm really sorry, Sam.' I gave him a pleading look and finally stopped to let him have his say.

185

He smiled reassuringly and he gently brushed a lock of hair away from my face.

'You've got nothing to be sorry about, Lucy. We're all afraid of something. That's one of the things that makes us who we are. And I love who you are. I love everything about you. Thank you for telling me about your fear. If I can help you in any way, I will. I wasn't making light of it. I know how awful it can make people feel. But I don't see why you think it might be a problem between us.'

'It's a problem if you want to go abroad. And I know how much you like travelling.'

His brows knit together. 'Why is it a problem? We can use the Channel tunnel if we want to go to Europe, and there are ferries to most places from there. It might take a little longer, but that means we'll have more time to spend together. That's not a problem. That's a blessing. Don't forget, I've taken my bike on most of my holidays. That's meant I couldn't go by plane, so you see, it really isn't an issue. And cruises aren't just for the elderly.' He slid his hands into my hair and eased my head towards his, that devastatingly gorgeous smile of his making my heart pound in my chest – but in a good way. A very good way. 'I love you, Lucy. Just being with you every day feels like a holiday.'

His kiss confirmed everything he'd just said and my heart soared with delight.

Sam truly loved me. And I truly loved him.

'Sam?' I asked, a few minutes later as our lips parted. 'What are you afraid of?'

He looked me in the eyes, his own eyes questioning.

'Afraid of?'

'You said we're all afraid of something.'

'Oh I see.' He smiled and then his expression was deadly serious. 'I'm afraid of losing you again.'

I beamed at him. 'You'll never lose me again.'

He breathed in deeply and then let out a slow sigh.

'I'm delighted to hear that,' he said huskily, his mouth within inches of mine once more. And then his tone changed and the serious expression was back. 'I'm afraid of clowns. I'm not joking. It's irrational, I know, but I can't help it. I had an unpleasant experience with a clown when I was a kid and even now I can't bear to be near one. They give me the creeps. Does that make you think less of me?'

'Absolutely not. I don't like clowns much either.'

'So we're agreed? No clowns at our kids' birthday parties.'

I gave a small gasp of delight. We were planning our future together and I couldn't have been happier.

'We're agreed. No clowns.'

'Because phobias are not a laughing matter,' he joked.

'They're not,' I confirmed as his mouth came down on mine in a kiss that was deep and passionate and made me feel as though I were flying among the stars. It was better than all the kisses we had shared all week.

I might have been afraid of getting on a plane but if that was what flying felt like, Sam Worth might be able to help me overcome my fears. With Sam by my side, I was sure that anything was possible.

And I was certain now, that despite us both having parents who were divorced – several times in his parents' case – Sam would be by my side for the rest of my life. And I would be by his.

The only problem, as far as I could see, was that I would need to persuade Erin that Sam would truly make me happy. I was sure as soon as she met him and saw us together, she would see how we felt about each other, so I wasn't really too concerned about that.

What did concern me, was how I was going to get my best friend to want to move to Fairlight Bay. But that was a problem for another day.

Coming soon

Visit www.emilyharvale.com to
see what's coming next.

Plus, sign up for Emily's newsletter, or
join her Facebook group, for all the latest
news about her books.

Stay in touch with

Emily Harvale

If you want to be the first to hear Emily's news, find out about book releases, see covers and help pick titles or names of characters, sign up to her newsletter.

visit: www.emilyharvale.com

Or join her Facebook group for all of the above and to chat with others about her books:

www.emilyharvale.com/FacebookGroup

Alternatively, just come and say 'Hello'
on social media:

 @EmilyHarvaleWriter

 @EmilyHarvale

 @EmilyHarvale

A Note from Emily

Thank you for reading this book. I really hope it brought a smile to your face. If so, I'd love it if you'd leave a short review on Amazon, or even just a rating.
And, maybe, tell your friends, or mention it on social media.

A little piece of my heart goes into all my books. I can't wait to bring you more stories that I hope will capture your heart, mind and imagination, allowing you to escape into a world of romance in some enticingly beautiful settings.

To see my books, or to sign up for my newsletter, please visit my website. The link is on the previous page.

I love chatting to readers, so pop over to Facebook or Instagram and say, 'Hello'. Or better yet, there's my lovely Facebook group for the latest book news, chats and general book-related fun. Again, you'll find details on the previous page.

Also by Emily Harvale

The Golf Widows' Club
Sailing Solo
Carole Singer's Christmas
Christmas Wishes
A Slippery Slope
The Perfect Christmas Plan
Be Mine
It Takes Two
Bells and Bows on Mistletoe Row

Lizzie Marshall series:
Highland Fling – book 1
Lizzie Marshall's Wedding – book 2

Goldebury Bay series:
Ninety Days of Summer – book 1
Ninety Steps to Summerhill – book 2
Ninety Days to Christmas – book 3

Hideaway Down series:
A Christmas Hideaway – book 1
Catch A Falling Star – book 2
Walking on Sunshine – book 3
Dancing in the Rain – book 4

Hall's Cross series
Deck the Halls – book 1
The Starlight Ball – book 2

Michaelmas Bay series
Christmas Secrets in Snowflake Cove – book 1
Blame it on the Moonlight – book 2

Friendships Blossom in Clementine Cove – book 3

Norman Landing series
Saving Christmas – book 1
A not so secret Winter Wedding – book 2
Sunsets and Surprises at Seascape Café – book 3
A Date at the end of The Pier – book 4

Locke Isle series
A Summer Escape – book 1
Christmas on Locke Isle – book 2

Betancourt Bay series
That Mistletoe Moment – book 1
That Winter Night – book 2
That Special Something – book 3
That Summer Hideaway – book 4
That Secret Wish – book 5

Midwinter Series
Christmas on Midwinter Lane – book 1
A Week in Midwinter – book 2

To see a complete list of my books, or to sign up for my newsletter, go to www.emilyharvale.com/books

There's also an exclusive Facebook group for fans of my books. www.emilyharvale.com/FacebookGroup

Or scan the QR code below to see all my books on Amazon.